'You're not af

'Should I be? Do
Kathryn challenge
wasn't in the least bit afraid of him.

'The idea becomes more enticing by the minute. Doesn't it?' Joel charged softly.

Warning bells went off in her head. 'I think this is where I should protest that we have only just met.'

'Maybe we have, but it only took a second for both of us to know we want each other.'

'Do we know it?' she charged mockingly, and he nodded.

'Oh, yes, and I give you fair warning, when I want something I usually get it.'

'Your arrogance is incredible!'

'My lovemaking is even better,' he retorted.

Amanda Browning still lives in the Essex house where she was born. The third of four children—her sister being her twin—she enjoyed the rough and tumble of life with two brothers as much as she did reading books. Writing came naturally as an outlet for a fertile imagination. The love of books led her to a career in libraries, and being single allowed her to take the leap into writing for a living. Success is still something of a wonder, but allows her to indulge in hobbies as varied as embroidery and bird-watching.

Recent titles by the same author:

THE PLAYBOY'S PROPOSAL

BY
AMANDA BROWNING

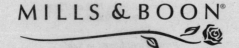

MILLS & BOON®

First published in Great Britain 2001
Harlequin Mills & Boon Limited,
Eton House, 18-24 Paradise Road, Richmond, Surrey TW9 1SR

© Amanda Browning 2001

ISBN 0 263 82519 1

Set in Times Roman 10½ on 12 pt.
01-0701-50636

Printed and bound in Spain
by Litografía Rosés, S.A., Barcelona

CHAPTER ONE

KATHRYN TEMPLETON was wrapped in a pleasant haze, floating somewhere between sleeping and waking. The virtually silent engine and the gentle music issuing from the car's speakers had had her sinking more comfortably into her seat and closing her eyes some time ago. It was the sudden cessation of noise as the music was turned off which brought her eyes open with a start, and she turned puzzled green orbs towards the driver, her Titian hair swinging about her face as she did so.

'What's up?' Glancing ahead, she expected to see trouble in the form of an accident, but the road, winding through a Lakeland landscape clad in a late-winter fall of snow, was empty.

'We're almost there,' declared Drew Templeton, her cousin and the reason she was sitting here heading into the Cumbrian wilds, as if that explained everything.

As far as Kathryn was concerned, it left a lot to be desired. Sitting up, she glanced at him curiously. 'So what's turned you so serious all of a sudden?'

Drew's fingers tapped out a nervy tattoo on the steering wheel. 'Nothing, really,' he denied, then added, 'I thought I'd better warn you about Joel, that's all.'

Finely arched brows rose questioningly in a heart-shaped face. Drew had been fairly reticent about his employer. All she knew was that he had trouble with his computer, and, because she cared for her cousin, she had agreed to help. She ran a small but flourishing business sorting out problems with computer programs.

'What about him?' It seemed to her a fine time to start issuing warnings, when they were almost at journey's end, but she guessed Drew hadn't wanted to risk her running out on him. The rat. Not that she would have. 'OK, tell me the worst. Is he some sort of monster?' she teased lightly, and he gave her a sombre look.

'Not exactly. I think the best way to describe Joel Kendrick is as a wolf in wolf's clothing,' he declared seriously.

The description had her ears pricking up. Really? She had never met an honest-to-goodness real life wolf before. What would he be like? Handsome, of course, with sex appeal dripping from every pore, or how else would he attract women? How did he go about seducing them? What, she wondered, with a quickening of her heart, would it be like flirting with him? The thought sent a tiny tremor of anticipation along her spine. There was nothing she enjoyed more than a light-hearted flirtation with a handsome, like-minded man. The weekend, which had offered only some interesting work, now took on a different complexion entirely. Smiling to herself, Kathryn folded her arms and gave Drew her full attention.

'How interesting. Do tell me more!' she invited with barely suppressed enthusiasm.

Her cousin groaned, not at all surprised by her response. Kathryn was cheerful and vivacious, and generally saw life as an adventure. Instead of viewing Joel Kendrick as someone to be avoided, she was more likely to see only the challenge of flirting with him. Unfortunately, his employer wasn't like most men she met. It worried him that there was a real danger here, and he didn't want to see her hurt.

'Listen, Kathy, I'm being serious. Joel is my em-

ployer, and I like him, but I don't have to approve of
his attitude towards the opposite sex. He has a predatory
eye for beautiful women. When he sees one he wants,
he goes after her with single-minded intent. Oh, he
treats his women well, but he's only interested in an
affair. Marriage is quite out of the question. Which, in-
cidentally, is why you're here.'

Far from being put off, Kathryn felt her curiosity
sharpen. 'You mean, one of his women caused this
computer malfunction?'

'Apparently she took exception to his ending their
affair, and we think she slipped back into the house
whilst he was out and deleted everything she could lay
her hands on. Then the system crashed, and.... Well,
this isn't my field. God knows what else she did, but
according to Joel it's a mess.'

'I see,' Kathryn mused, silently praising the woman's
ingenuity. It certainly beat cutting his suits to shreds.
The woman had style.

Drew sighed and flicked on the indicator before turning off the main road. 'Joel called me and asked if I
knew anyone who could help. He doesn't want just anyone raking around in his business. I knew I could trust
you, but it wasn't until we were on our way that I realised taking you to Joel was like throwing you to the
wolf.'

'Because you think he might be interested in adding
me to his list of conquests?' Kathryn enquired teasingly,
and Drew turned troubled eyes on her.

'You certainly fit his criteria.'

She grinned. This was sounding very promising,
'You mean I'm breathing?' she taunted wryly.

'I mean, you're beautiful,' Drew corrected heavily,
and she quickly reached out and squeezed his arm.

'Thank you for the compliment,' she said warmly, and, unable to resist her patent affection, he grinned back at her.

'You're entirely welcome.'

Sitting back in her seat, Kathryn studied the starkly beautiful landscape. They were on a lakeside road, and the view was breathtaking. She liked winter. Everything seemed so sharp and clean. Eventually, though, her thoughts turned back to Joel Kendrick.

It was as well he wasn't looking for a wife, because he didn't sound her type at all. She was looking for that one man she would want to spend the rest of her life with. She knew that one day she would meet a man and fall in love with him in an instant, because love was like that. Whilst she waited, though, she wasn't averse to having some fun. So what if Drew's boss wasn't husband material? As a diversion he fitted the bill nicely. She was well and truly intrigued by the possibility of indulging in some fascinating exchanges with a man who must have flirtation down to a fine art. Really, Drew needn't worry about her being seduced by this latter-day Casanova. She had her head screwed on, and wasn't about to become Joel Kendrick's next conquest.

'So, Joel Kendrick is used to getting any woman he wants, is he?' she mused thoughtfully.

'Being handsome and rich has something to do with it. Women seem to fall for him in droves,' Drew added dryly.

'Ah, the pull of sex appeal.'

She knew its power. Had fallen under its spell once or twice in her search for love and Mr Right. She knew she was as susceptible as the next woman when it came to a hunky male, but that didn't mean she gave in to it.

She had had a grand total of two relationships in her twenty-six years. It was no hardship to keep her relationships platonic. Sex for sex's sake had never had an appeal.

'What does he do? I mean, he doesn't simply chase women all day, does he?'

'He's a business man, with engineering companies worldwide. He can be ruthless at times, but he's well respected in the City. He took over the original company when his father retired, and has taken it from strength to strength. He's a force to be reckoned with, but unfortunately it means he's used to getting his own way.'

So, he was a strong-willed man. Well, she was used to strong-willed men. Her father and brothers were such men, with a tendency to issue commands to the youngest child and only daughter because they loved her and wanted to protect her. She understood that, but never let them ride roughshod over her. Consequently, their battles had become legendary. She was, after all, her father's daughter, and equally strong-willed.

'Do you honestly think I'm likely to be interested in him?'

'I hope not,' Drew responded fervently. There was no knowing quite which way Kathryn would go, but a prudent man expected the worst. He pulled a face. 'Though it's been my experience that women can't seem to help themselves where he's concerned.'

She laughed wryly, easily following his line of thought. The trouble with Drew was that he knew her too well. 'Thanks for the vote of confidence. As it happens, I'm no push-over. Have you given thought to the possibility that *I* might not like *him*?' The law of prob-

ability said that there must be some women who were
immune to his practised charm.

'No. You'd do something silly just for fun even if
you didn't like him. Just don't get involved with him,'
Drew commanded. 'Be kind to yourself, Kathy. He's
not the sort of man you want to play around with.'

There was no doubting his concern, and she loved
him for it, but she felt he was rather jumping the gun.
OK, she was thinking of sharpening her claws a little,
but she could always change her mind. 'I tell you what,
I'll take it under advisement. For now, I think I'll just
reserve judgement. After all, I haven't even met the
man!'

A situation which was about to be remedied some
fifteen minutes later, when Drew brought the car to a
halt before a large stone-built house, with gables and an
extra wing tacked on to one end of it.

'So, this is the wolf's lair?' Kathryn declared, tongue
very firmly in cheek, as she climbed out of the car. It
was beautiful.

Drew retrieved their luggage from the boot. 'Come
and meet him. I hope you've got some garlic handy.'

'Silly, that's only good against vampires. What I need
is a silver bullet, and I'm fresh out of those. I'll put
them on my shopping list.'

'You may joke now,' Drew responded, seeing her
determination to make light of the situation as a bad
sign. 'I only hope you don't end up laughing on the
other side of your face.'

Kathryn slipped an arm through his and squeezed
gently. 'Don't worry, Drew. I can take care of myself.'

He looked at her doubtfully. 'Hmm. Famous last
words. Oh, well, I've had my say. It's up to you now.'

The sound of footsteps came from inside as Kathryn

replied, 'I'm a big girl. I had my twenty-sixth birthday a month ago, remember.'

'I know; I was there. And, I'm happy to say, you were very well behaved. Perhaps you are getting some sense after all. Am I being overprotective?'

She smiled at him. 'Just a bit, but you're allowed.'

'It's just that with my flying off to Germany tomorrow I won't be here to protect you.'

Would her family ever stop protecting her? she wondered wryly. 'Stop worrying. I'll be fine. But if worse comes to worse, I'll let you say I told you so.'

The door opened before Drew could respond by telling her it didn't make him feel any better. Framed in the doorway, a cheerful woman in her sixties smiled warmly at them.

'Good afternoon, Mr Templeton. You made good time, then?' she greeted Drew, and nodded at Kathryn, stepping back so that they could enter.

'I thought it best not to keep him waiting, Agnes. Didn't want to make him testy,' Drew said, urging Kathryn inside ahead of him, where the warmth enveloped them both. 'Agnes is Joel's housekeeper, and all-round good egg. This is my cousin Kathryn. She's come to the rescue.'

The older woman looked at Kathryn more closely and her face fell comically. 'Oh dear,' she said faintly, and Kathryn frowned in ready concern.

'Is something wrong?'

'Not at all, my dear,' Agnes denied as she closed the front door. 'You're very welcome, I'm sure. It's just....you're very pretty.'

'Ah,' said Kathryn, seeing the light, and couldn't help laughing, though not unkindly. 'It's all right, Agnes. Drew has told me all about our furry friend.'

'Furry friend?' It was the housekeeper's turn to look puzzled.

Kathryn leant down towards the woman, who was a good half a head shorter. 'The wolf,' she whispered confidentially. 'Don't worry, I had a tetanus booster not long ago.'

'Just lead us to him, Agnes,' her cousin suggested, setting their bags at the foot of the stairs and removing his coat. He handed it to the housekeeper and Kathryn did the same. 'My cousin has a weird sense of humour. Don't try to understand her.'

Agnes, far from being put out, suddenly had a twinkle in her eye. 'Something tells me somebody might just have met his match. You're not at all what he was expecting. For one thing, he was expecting a man. You'll find him in the library, gnashing his teeth and cursing till the air is blue. I'll bring along some coffee in a few minutes. Unless you would prefer something else?'

Kathryn said coffee was fine, and Drew led the way to the back of the house, then along a passage to the west wing. As he opened the door, Kathryn felt her heart rate increase in sudden expectation, and smoothed the blue chenille jumper she wore with leggings down over her hips. As she followed her cousin inside, she heard a husky voice growl a greeting.

'It's about damn time you got here!' it said, and she grimaced. It sounded very much as if the wolf had a sore head.

She almost felt sorry for him. Almost. Stepping inside, she caught her first glimpse of the man she had heard so much about.

Joel Kendrick was certainly impressive. He stood by the fireplace, where a fire blazed welcomingly, a glass of what appeared to be whisky in his hand. He was a tall man, broad-shouldered and slim-hipped, and clearly at the peak of fitness. He wore jeans which hugged his long muscular legs, and a black sweater which outlined a powerfully masculine physique. He was somewhere in his mid-thirties, she guessed, with hair so dark it appeared blue where the light caught it. His face, even from the side, was most definitely handsome, but there was a ruggedness about it which prevented it from being too pretty.

There was no denying it; he was a very attractive man. In fact, he was the most attractive man she had seen in a long while. She could feel the aura of him even from where she stood, and rather unexpectedly it set her nerve-endings tingling like crazy. Even stationary he had a kind of dynamic magnetism which reached across the space separating them and touched her. At its basic level, it was the female responding to a prime example of the male of the species. Translated to the present day, it meant she could no more ignore him than she could stop breathing.

It wasn't at all what she'd been expecting, but she wasn't overly alarmed by it. On the contrary, it added a certain spice to the situation. It was time to make her presence felt.

'As we didn't have Scotty to beam us through the air in a split nanosecond, I think we did a pretty good job getting here so quickly,' she put in before Drew could utter a word, and instantly found herself staring into piercing blue eyes.

They were the sort of eyes which, in certain circumstances, would create havoc with a woman's senses, and when they locked with hers that was precisely what they did. Because something elemental connected them in the space of a heartbeat. The air seemed to sizzle and hum between them, as if it had taken a positive charge. It was pure chemistry, and a look was all it had taken to set off a chain reaction. The attraction was instant—and mutual.

Kathryn experienced a familiar curling sensation inside her. She acknowledged it with a shiver of excitement. Attraction, pure but not so simple. Just as she had supposed, the man had sex appeal oozing from every pore, and it had struck her on a primitive level. Her senses responded by setting every nerve in her body tingling. Given his visual attraction, she wasn't surprised to feel it, but she was surprised by its strength. The man had something, and whatever it was her senses liked it. Liked it a lot.

His eyes as they roved over her were like a lick of flame, and she wondered if it had been wise to wear leggings tucked into knee-length boots for the journey. It showed off altogether too much of her to his gaze. Not that she revealed her concern for an instant. Every instinct she possessed told her that he was not the sort of man you gave any sort of weapon to.

'And you are?' Joel Kendrick asked curiously, in a voice laced with a lethal brand of husky sensuality. Setting his glass aside, he slipped his hands into the pockets of his jeans, a move which tightened the material around his thighs and raised her temperature accordingly.

The man was pure dynamite, she acknowledged wryly, and all done without even trying. It was stunning. Nobody had had quite this effect on her before. How could she possibly ignore it? Did she want to? That imp of devilment which was always under indifferent control now decided to come to the surface, and, as Drew had feared, she didn't resist it.

'I'm the woman you've been waiting for,' she quipped back with a deliberate mix of seduction and mockery.

Amusement flickered in those devilish blue eyes. 'Is that so?' he drawled softly, giving her his full attention in a way that set up goosebumps on her flesh.

Caught between them, Drew rolled his eyes despairingly. 'Kathryn, cut it out!' he ordered.

'Shut up, Drew,' Joel commanded quietly, strolling towards her. 'This is just getting interesting.' Coming to a halt a mere foot away, he smiled lazily, an action that threatened to steal her breath away. 'So, I've been waiting for you, have I?'

She inclined her head, smiling sweetly, whilst her heart raced away at a mile a minute at his closeness. 'Impatiently, by the sounds of it.'

He shrugged that off without taking his eyes from her. 'My temper's been a bit frayed lately, but it's improving by leaps and bounds now.'

Kathryn laughed, a sultry sound that made something flare to life in the depths of his eyes. 'I have that effect on people.' She knew she was behaving outrageously, but she couldn't seem to help herself. 'In fact, they've been known to hug and kiss me on sight.'

He grinned, and there was definitely something wolfish about it. 'I can quite see why. I'm tempted to do the same.'

Oh, boy, he had the charisma to make a woman forget her principles just when she ought to be standing on them, she decided as she held up an admonitory hand to keep him at bay. 'I should wait until you've seen what I can do first.'

Joel laughed, sending a tingle down her spine and curling her toes. 'I'm impressed already.'

Drew, by this time, had steam coming out of his ears. He crossed over to them and took Kathryn by the arm. 'OK, that's enough!' he exclaimed, and she turned startled eyes on him, having quite forgotten he was there. 'When you've quite finished playing games, perhaps I should introduce you.'

A faint flush skimmed her cheeks, but it had nothing to do with his remonstration. She mouthed the word 'sorry' to him. It was partly true. She was sorry for upsetting him, but not for behaving as she had. It had been fun. It had been exciting. Her heart was still tripping madly, with no sign of slowing. Boy, the man was positively lethal. He had switched her senses on like a neon light. So that was what it felt like to flirt with the world's number one playboy! It could become addictive. Already she wanted more.

Drew, meanwhile, was making the promised introductions. 'Joel, this is my cousin, Kathryn Templeton. She's here to sort out your computer for you.'

Joel's eyes immediately narrowed on her thoughtfully. 'Ah, now I get it. That's what makes you the woman I've been waiting for.'

'Impatiently,' she added for good measure, laughing into his eyes.

He took a deep breath, which expanded his chest magnificently. 'Well, let's hope you're as good with bits and bytes as you are with words, Kathryn Templeton.'

Another laugh escaped her. 'With all modesty I can say I'm better.'

One eyebrow quirked lazily. 'All modesty? You don't believe in hiding your light under a bushel?'

She shrugged and exchanged a knowing look with her cousin. 'In my family you have to fight your corner or sink without trace. I don't intend to be the next *Titanic*.'

'Competitive, are they, your family?'

'Like you wouldn't believe. I have four older brothers,' she admitted, not to mention her father. She tucked her arm through Drew's. 'This side of the Templeton clan is protective and supportive without being combative, I'm happy to say.'

Joel rubbed his chin wryly. 'Which means he's probably warned you about the Big Bad Wolf.'

'Of course. He doesn't want to see me devoured like Red Riding Hood,' she responded brightly.

Joel looked amused. 'Something tells me if I tried it, I'd probably get indigestion.'

'I'm certainly too rich for some people's taste,' Kathryn agreed breezily.

'An acquired taste?'

'Absolutely.'

His expression revealing equal amounts of intrigue and appreciation, Joel Kendrick held out his hand. 'It's a pleasure to make your acquaintance, Kathryn Templeton,' he declared, his voice again carrying that husky sensuality which found its mark and set the nerves in her stomach quivering.

Nonetheless, she smiled back. 'Likewise, Mr Kendrick,' she returned smartly.

'Joel,' he prompted with a decided gleam in his eye as she took his hand.

'Joel,' she repeated obediently, a cool smile hovering about her lips.

What happened next rocked her belief in her ability to remain detached and in control. As their hands touched, she looked into those wickedly alluring, fathomless blue eyes and found herself drowning in them.

For an instant she lost her bearings entirely. Her nervous system went into overload and her breath got lodged in her throat, so that she forgot to breathe. The swiftness of her response to him was stunning. She had felt sexual attraction before, but never experienced quite this brand of magnetic potency. It drew her as nothing else had. Sensible thought was vanquished by a tidal wave of sensuality. In the flicker of a heartbeat she wanted him. Craved him like a hungry woman craved food, and her body swayed towards him, seeking appeasement. Seeking...

The sound of a polite cough gathered her scattered wits into a seething whole, and Kathryn careened back into the present with a gasp. She had an instant to see the answering passion in those blue eyes before the instinct of self-preservation took over and she swiftly hid her thoughts behind practised calm. She eased her hand away just as Agnes brought in a tray of coffee, and she turned to the woman, grateful for the breathing space.

Joel Kendrick had proved to be more than a little overwhelming close up. Always before she had had the ability to keep a cool head, but this man had changed that completely. It shook her, and sent a frisson of alarm through her system. Drew was right, this man was different. She had an inkling of what he could do to her, and it was distinctly unsettling.

'Can I help you with that, Agnes?' she asked in a voice that thankfully gave away nothing of her inner turmoil.

The housekeeper smiled at her. 'Thank you, my dear. If you'd just move that vase to one side... There.' She set the tray down whilst Kathryn found another spot for the vase. When she straightened up, she glanced at Drew. 'Have you eaten, Mr Templeton?'

'Not since this morning, Agnes,' Drew admitted.

It was a cue for Kathryn to shoot Joel a mocking look. She might be all of a twitter inside, but not for the world would she let anyone know it, least of all the cause. Keeping up the appearance of normality was suddenly very important. Having started out flirtatiously, she couldn't now back off without giving too much away.

'He said we couldn't spare the time. Food was weighed in the balance against your temper, and found wanting,' she taunted gently, not averse to saying what she thought. She was here to do him a favour. Her livelihood didn't rest upon his goodwill. Besides, she felt the need to goad him a little, because the best form of defence was often attack. Until she had had time to think, it seemed the most appropriate thing to do.

Joel's response was to raise an eyebrow, but he said nothing to her, merely turned to his housekeeper. 'You'd better bring dinner forward, Agnes. I'd hate to see such a beautiful woman fainting away.'

'Very good, Master Joel,' Agnes agreed. 'I've put Mr Templeton in his usual room, and I thought it best to put the young lady in the rose room.'

Joel's expression became wry, but he smiled fondly at the elderly woman. 'Quite right. The rose room does have some of the best views.'

'And it's on the other side of the house from you,' Agnes added pointedly, causing Kathryn to hastily smother a laugh. 'Now, if you'd give me a hand with the cases, Mr Templeton, I can get the food on the table sooner,' she declared in her motherly fashion, and bustled out again.

'*Master* Joel?' Kathryn asked in amusement, after Drew had obediently followed the other woman from the room. She had recovered her equilibrium, and felt more able to hold her own with him now that her pulse had steadied.

Joel pulled a wry face. 'Agnes used to be my nanny. She's been with my family for many years, and nobody wanted to see her go, so her position has changed several times. She was companion to my mother before becoming my housekeeper. She's more like one of the family now.'

Kathryn felt a curl of warmth grow inside her at his explanation. It showed, she was glad to notice, that there was a softer side to him. 'I like that.' Her grandfather, her mother's father, treated his servants as something below his notice. His only interest in their welfare was in how it would affect him.

'You approve?'

'I always approve of kindness. My grandfather would call it foolish sentimentality,' she admitted regretfully. 'You don't keep somebody on when they're past their usefulness.'

'Your grandfather, if you'll forgive me for saying so, is a fool.'

Kathryn smiled wryly. 'Blunt, but true. He's a cold man. I'll never understand how my grandmother came to marry him, but it's no mystery to me why she left. I'm very like her, so I'm told.'

Joel raised an eyebrow questioningly. 'Don't you know?'

'He won't have a picture of her in the house,' she explained evenly. 'She humiliated him, you see, by leaving. I used to think the reason he didn't like me was because I reminded him of her.' Childhood visits to her grandfather's house had been far from pleasant.

'But you don't think that now?'

She smiled and shook her head. 'The truth is it isn't in him to love or be loved.'

'Whereas you are eminently loveable,' he declared with a decidedly rakish gleam lighting up his eyes again.

Barely recovered from the last time, the nerves in Kathryn's stomach quivered in reaction, but she laughed and shot him an old-fashioned look. 'Do you think flattery is going to get you somewhere?' she asked, sounding far too breathless to her own ears, but thankfully Joel didn't appear to notice.

His grin was charmingly lopsided. 'A man has to live in hope.'

Kathryn groaned silently. Everything about him pleased her rioting senses. It was amazing she was still on her feet, considering her knees felt like jelly. Still she battled on. Tipping her head to one side, she eyed him thoughtfully. 'Are you really as good as they say you are?'

He placed a hand on his chest, whilst a smile flickered round the edges of his mouth. 'In all humility, I couldn't possibly say.'

Oh, Lord, just let me get through the next few minutes without turning into a gibbering idiot, she prayed silently, as the power of his charm hit her yet more devastatingly. 'Meaning, if I want to know, I'll have to find out for myself?'

His shrug was careless, but his eyes glittered invitingly. 'There's nothing to compare with first-hand knowledge. You might find it...interesting.'

She was sure she would. This was seduction on the grand scale, and, despite her floundering senses, she met it with a gurgling laugh. 'I'm sure it would be educational, but there's always the danger of the commodity being overpriced.'

'Trust me,' Joel urged throatily. 'I always do my very best to give value for money.'

'Hmm,' she murmured consideringly, whilst the nerves in her stomach fluttered around like demented butterflies. Oh, he was good. He was very good. All he'd done was utter a few innuendoes and she was quivering like a jelly because her mind had filled in the gaps with vivid pictures that definitely needed censoring.

'I've a feeling the woman who mashed your computer felt just a little short-changed,' she observed ironically, and Joel's smile vanished like magic. She blinked, surprised to find she had hit a nerve. So the man was vulnerable after all.

'She took the relationship too seriously,' he declared shortly, and Kathryn's heart lurched as she took in the message. She knew it wasn't specifically aimed at her, but it might as well have been. Her nerves steadied as she heeded the warning shot across her bows.

'Perhaps she didn't intend to. Perhaps she fell in love with you,' she suggested, and her lips parted on a soft gasp as her statement brought a chilly glitter to his eyes.

'I didn't ask her to,' he added grimly, and she laughed chidingly,

'Nobody asks to fall in love, they just do,' she argued, stating what most people accepted as universal, but Joel looked at her steadily.

'I don't, and I never intend to. I make no secret of it.'

Kathryn felt a chill wind brush past her and shivered faintly because he had sounded so adamant. 'How can you be so certain you'll never fall in love?' she asked curiously. It seemed to her a rash statement to make.

'Because in order for it to happen you have to believe in it, and I don't believe in love,' he told her firmly, but she saw the flaw in his argument immediately.

'You love Agnes,' she said softly, and his eyes narrowed.

'That's different. The kind of love we're talking about between a man and a woman doesn't exist.'

The flat statement, in direct opposition to her own belief, couldn't pass without argument. 'There are countless millions of people out there who would disagree with you. They can't all be wrong.'

He dismissed them, and her, with a shrug. 'If they want to believe in fairy tales, I won't stop them.'

Kathryn shook her head sadly. 'You know, beliefs like that are likely to get shot down in flames. It wouldn't surprise me if one day love hit you right between the eyes and proved you wrong.'

Joel laughed out loud, his good humour restored as quickly as it had departed. 'I won't be holding my breath. And don't you let those rose-coloured glasses of yours trip you up. I wouldn't want to see all that beauty spoilt.'

Kathryn smiled at him confidently. 'It won't be. You see, I happen to believe the man for me is out there somewhere. I just haven't met him yet.'

'And in the meantime?'

She laughed, her shrug a masterful touch. 'In the meantime, I enjoy searching, because there are interesting stops along the way.'

He stepped heart-stoppingly closer. 'Like coming here to sort out my computer?'

His closeness didn't make thinking easier. Still, she managed to find a chirpy reply. 'Exactly. If I hadn't said I'd help Drew, who knows when I would have met another Big Bad Wolf?'

'You're not afraid of me?'

'Should I be? Do you intend to devour me?' she challenged scoffingly, knowing she wasn't the least bit afraid of him.

The fires in his eyes sent out sparks. 'The idea becomes more enticing by the minute. Doesn't it?' he charged softly, the question heavy with meaning, and her breath caught as her stomach twisted with a powerful surge of desire.

Her lips trembled faintly, drawing his eyes. Crazy as it was, her flesh tingled as if he had actually touched her. Warning bells went off in her head. 'I think this is where I should protest that we have only just met.'

Reaching out, he drew a finger lightly across her lips, setting up a tingle she felt to her core. 'Maybe we have, but it took only a second for both of us to know we want each other.'

Without warning he had brought the unspoken out into the open and her brows rose. Instinct put her on the defensive. '*Do* we know it?' she charged mockingly, and he nodded.

'Oh, yes, and I give you fair warning. When I want something, I usually get it.'

Her throat closed over and she had to swallow hard to answer. 'It never does anyone any good to get everything they want,' she pointed out with creditable calmness.

His smile was pure seduction. 'Resist it if you want. It makes victory even sweeter.'

Her heart tripped. Like a big cat sensing its prey's vulnerability, he was trying to outflank her. She couldn't allow that to happen. 'Such confidence! You could lose, you know.'

'I could, but I'm going to do everything in my power to ensure that I don't.'

Kathryn gasped. 'Your arrogance is incredible!'

'My lovemaking is better,' he returned sexily, and sent her defences scattering to the four winds.

Wow! This man had all the weapons, and then some. Taking a steadying breath, Kathryn urged her fluttering heart to be still. Drew was right; this man was dangerous. If he could make her defences crumble without really trying, what would happen if and when he did try? It was more than time to beat a strategic retreat.

'I'll have to take your word on that. For the moment I'm more interested in freshening up before dinner. Agnes has put me in the rose room, isn't that right?' she said, with all the composure she could muster.

'This time I'll let you run away, but it won't always be so. Left at the top of the stairs and follow your nose. You can't miss it. No doubt Agnes will have fitted the steel door by now in an attempt to keep me out,' he added sardonically, and Kathryn left the room feeling as if she had been put through a wringer.

Events had taken an unexpected turn. This was not how she had foreseen the weekend going. Joel had turned her world on its head, and she found herself in a situation entirely new to her. Joel Kendrick wanted her and she wanted him. The problem was, she had never entered into a relationship that had no happy ending in sight. And that, if she responded to the way he could make her feel, was what she would have to do. He had made that very clear. From nowhere, she found herself with some serious decisions to make, and very little time to make them.

CHAPTER TWO

UPSTAIRS in her bedroom, Kathryn sank down onto the bed and gave her wobbly legs a much needed rest. She felt shattered and intoxicated in equal quantities. Nothing could have adequately prepared her for meeting Joel Kendrick. No advance warnings could have equipped her for the reality. She had thought to have some fun, and certainly hadn't expected to be attracted to him so strongly, or to have that attraction reciprocated.

What she felt went way beyond anything in her experience. She could honestly say she had never felt such an intense physical attraction. It was there between them like a living, breathing thing. What did she do about it? That was the question. She knew what Joel wanted, but what did *she* want?

To have an affair with Joel would no doubt be an incredible experience, but it would break her own rules, because if he were to be believed—and she had no reason to doubt him—there was no future in it. She might like to flirt, but she wasn't a fool. She never went further unless she thought there might be a future with the man.

Only, there was a part of her which said this time was special. That she would be a fool to turn it down. Yet if she took what was on offer, that would be doing what Drew had said, and throwing herself to the wolf. Would being part of his life for a brief time be worth it? Certainly she wouldn't know unless she tried it. But she was only here for two days. Two days wouldn't even amount to an affair. It would be, at best, a brief encounter. Surely she had more respect for herself than to give in to her passions for a mere forty-eight hours?

With a heavy sigh she fell back onto the bed, knowing the answer. Common sense said it had to be no. She mustn't allow herself more than a brief flirtation. At least she had an inkling of just how dangerous he could be to her if she wasn't careful. She was going to have to keep her wits about her, for she didn't doubt for a moment that he would take advantage of their mutual attraction. His reputation was proof enough. Pride dictated that she must not become his next conquest, no matter how strong the pull on her senses.

A soft knock on the door brought her up on her elbow.

'Who is it?'

'Drew,' the muffled voice responded, and she grimaced, knowing what was coming.

'Come in,' she invited, scrambling to the side of the bed and swinging her legs down.

Drew looked at her closely as he entered and shut the door, and she wondered what he expected to see.

'It's OK, you don't have to say it, I know,' she declared wryly, hoping to head him off at the pass. No such luck.

Her cousin came and sat beside her, concern heavy on his brow. 'What were you thinking of?' he challenged despairingly, and that brought a smile to her lips.

'It wasn't the sort of situation where thinking came into it,' she returned wryly. She had simply responded to the signals coming off Joel, and her own rioting senses.

'Kathy, this man could break your heart.'

Reaching for Drew's hand, she squeezed it reassuringly. 'Don't worry. I'm not going to let him. I have no intention of being seduced.'

'But you are attracted to him?' Drew persisted, and she shrugged fatalistically.

'I won't deny it. He's a very attractive man. But I'm not stupid, Drew. I know where to draw the line.'

He didn't look totally convinced, but grudgingly accepted what she said with a proviso. 'Just make sure Joel knows where the line is, too.'

Kathryn stood up and tugged him to his feet. 'Oh, I intend to. Now, get out of here and let me freshen up. I'm starving, and the smells wafting up are making my stomach rumble. Besides, if I'm quick, I could get a look at that computer before dinner. The sooner I start, the sooner I can be finished and on my way home.'

That clearly met with his approval, and he went without further comment, leaving Kathryn to sigh heavily. Then, because she was a practical person, not given to languishing on thoughts of what might have been, she gathered together her sponge bag and a change of clothes and went in search of the bathroom.

As it turned out, Kathryn didn't get an opportunity to look over Joel's computer until after dinner. When she went back downstairs, this time dressed in a long-sleeved holly-green dress made of soft wool, she met Agnes coming from the dining room.

'My, don't you look nice this evening, miss,' the housekeeper declared with a warm smile.

Kathryn smiled back. 'Thank you, Agnes. Something smells good.'

'Lancashire hotpot. Master Joel's favourite. The table's set, so it won't be more than a few minutes now.

If you go into the sitting room, you can help yourself to a drink before dinner,' Agnes suggested, pointing to a door on the other side of the hall.

Realising her hope of looking over the computer had to be abandoned, Kathryn obediently made her way to the sitting room. It was a pleasant room, with comfortable sofas and armchairs surrounding the brick fireplace where another fire blazed cheerfully. Drinks were set on a tray on the sideboard, and Kathryn helped herself to a small Martini. If she wanted to get some work done later, drinking too much now would be inadvisable.

She was studying a group of photos on the mantelpiece when a subtle shift of the air told her Joel had come into the room. She had never been so attuned to a man that she could sense his presence even at a distance. It was uncanny, and she didn't know quite what to make of it. Turning, she found him just inside the door, studying her with eyes that gleamed appreciatively. In response, her nerves took a tiny leap and set her pulse throbbing. He looked magnificent, and her heart did a crazy lurch as her own eyes ate him up. The white silk shirt and black trousers he now wore barely seemed to tame him. He moved, coming towards her with a lithe, pantherish grace that tightened her stomach with desire.

'You look good enough to eat,' he murmured, his gaze setting her nerves alight with such disconcerting ease it was a wonder she didn't melt on the spot.

'I thought hotpot was your favourite,' she countered, far too breathlessly for comfort, and he was smiling softly as he looked deeply into her eyes.

'When it comes to food, yes. However, the appetite you arouse will settle for nothing less than your presence in my bed.'

It was heady stuff on an empty stomach, and she groaned silently, aware that her body responded to every soft word with a will of its own. Still, she had made her decision and would stick to it.

'If you check with the management, I think you'll find I'm not on the menu,' she returned smoothly, watching the way his eyes crinkled at the corners when his smile deepened.

He bent towards her confidingly. 'Could you really watch me starve?' he taunted softly, and she raised an eyebrow quizzically.

'Somehow, I don't think you'd starve for long,' she quipped, and strangely enough it hurt to say it, which was odd, for she had always known she was not important to him. She was no more than a passing fancy because she was here.

'Ah, but sometimes hunger can only be satisfied by one thing—or one woman,' Joel insisted softly.

Kathryn took a steadying sip of her drink, fearing he was right. He had come out with all guns blazing this evening, and the attack on her defences were definitely weakening them. She needed the drink to strengthen her resolve.

'But hunger is such a contrary thing. Now it wants one thing; next time it wants something completely different,' she countered, but he shook his head.

'Not always. Sometimes it takes a very long time for hunger to be satisfied.'

'Just not for ever,' Kathryn shot back pointedly, and he acknowledged the hit with an inclination of his head.

'No, not for ever. Everything diminishes in time,' Joel agreed as he wandered over to the drinks tray and poured himself a small whisky. Sipping it, he looked at her over the glass.

'There is an exception, though I hesitate to mention it, knowing your opinion of love,' Kathryn reminded him, and he lowered the glass.

'Do you really think this love you believe in lasts for ever?' he asked curiously.

'It can do, but it has to be worked at. You can't ever take it for granted, but the more you feed it the more it grows,' she said with utter conviction, and that brought a tiny frown to his forehead.

'You can say that, even though your own grandparents' marriage failed?'

She sighed. He had to pick on the one failure to illustrate his case, but his argument was based on a false premise. 'The marriage failed because there was only love on one side. My mother has told me many times that my grandmother loved my grandfather; she just couldn't live with his coldness.' Left alone with her father, it hadn't been easy for her mother either. In the end it had driven Lucy Makepeace to find a place of her own to live as soon as she was old enough.

'What happened to your grandmother?' Joel asked conversationally, sliding one hand casually into the pocket of his trousers.

The question caught her off-guard, allowing the old sadness to show in her eyes as she frowned. 'I really don't know. There was a messy divorce and a bitter custody battle, which my grandfather won, and that was the last anyone ever saw of her,' she revealed with a faint shrug of her shoulders.

'You miss her?' Joel asked curiously, and Kathryn sighed heavily, because her feelings concerning the situation were more complex than a simple answer could convey.

'It's hard to miss someone you never knew. What I

miss is not having known her. The person she was. There is so much about her I want to know,' she said honestly, and her smile was deprecating. 'I guess I want to ask her why she never came to see my mother. I can't ask my grandfather because he never speaks of her. It's a mystery I don't know how to solve.'

'Have you never tried to trace her?'

Kathryn shook her head. 'I wouldn't know where to start,' she declared wistfully, then, because thinking of her grandmother always left her dissatisfied, she made a determined effort to lift her spirits. 'What about you? Are both your parents living?'

'Oh, yes. They're still going strong, and seem younger than ever, even though they celebrated their golden wedding last year. At present they're in Canada, visiting relatives. Then they're off to Hawaii,' Joel confirmed, and she tipped her head to one side thoughtfully.

'So they weren't the ones who made you so cynical about love. That means it has to be a woman,' she mused, watching him carefully. But, as she was coming to expect, he gave nothing away.

Instead one eyebrow lifted lazily. 'You think so?'

Kathryn laughed softly. 'It has to be, and you haven't denied it. What did she do? Leave you for another man?'

Joel shook his head. 'She couldn't, as she's nothing but a figment of your imagination.'

Her eyes narrowed as she tossed that around in her mind. 'Hmm, I see. That's very interesting. If it wasn't one woman, then it has to be all women. What do we fail to do that convinces you love doesn't exist?' She posed the question to herself, and almost immediately saw the answer. 'We don't see you as just a man, do we? All we see is a bank balance. An unending source of spending money. That's it, isn't it?' she charged him, convinced she was right.

In response, Joel drained his glass and set it aside. When he looked at her again, there was a dangerous glitter in his eyes. 'You're very perceptive.'

'That's because I have a similar problem. My father is a very wealthy man, and I'm his only daughter. Which makes me an heiress set to inherit a fortune, and a prime target. There are a lot of men out there who would like to get their hands on the money they think I'll get one day,' Kathryn returned with a grimace of distaste.

'And yet you still believe in fairy stories,' Joel remarked scornfully, and she tilted her chin upwards defiantly.

'That's because I know all men are not the same. Neither are all women.'

He came to her then, his hand reaching out to cup her chin. 'That hasn't been my experience. I prefer to believe in what I know exists: desire. Love is a fallacy; sexual attraction is real. You feel it. Right now your heart is beating just a little bit faster, isn't it? I can see that delicious pulse throbbing in your throat. It's urging me to kiss it. To know the feel and taste of you,' he whispered huskily, his eyes glowing with a fierce heat as they looked into hers.

Kathryn's heart lurched in response to the siren call of his desire. She wanted him to do it, too. Her flesh seemed to scream out for it, and it was incredibly painful to step back away from him, forcing his hand to drop to his side.

'I hardly think this is the time or the place for what you have in mind,' she told him sardonically, and he smiled faintly.

'Nevertheless, you felt it. You felt the hunger.'

Oh, boy, had she! Her whole body was still pulsating with it. 'Maybe I did, but right now I have a more urgent hunger that needs satisfying. I haven't eaten all day,' she protested, seeking to bring some order to the sensual chaos she felt whenever he was near.

Joel laughed wryly. 'Then we must deal with that one first. The other will be all the better for waiting.'

'What will be better?' Drew enquired idly as he strolled into the room, looking from one to the other questioningly.

Kathryn felt colour heat her cheeks, aware that if he had arrived a few minutes sooner he would have walked in on quite a different scenario, and she wouldn't have heard the last of it.

'Dinner,' she explained with feigned nonchalance. 'I was just saying I hadn't eaten all day. I'm starving.'

'Me, too,' Drew agreed, and as if to underline the fact his stomach rumbled audibly.

'Help yourself to a drink, Drew,' Joel invited with a laugh. 'I'll just go and see what's keeping Agnes.'

Drew followed the suggestion, but turned to his cousin the instant they were alone. 'Dinner?' he challenged with an old-fashioned look.

Kathryn stared him out, her chin raised. 'What else?' she countered, daring him to argue, but Drew, for once, wisely decided to hold his own counsel. She drained her glass and was tempted to refill it. Joel had won round one on points; she could only hope to do better in round two.

Dinner was every bit as delicious as it had promised to be. The meat and vegetables were cooked to perfection, and there was fresh crusty bread to go with it. The two men spent most of the meal discussing Drew's trip to Germany tomorrow, and Kathryn was happy to be left alone. She found herself watching Joel with fascination. Even talking business, he had an animation about him that held her rapt. She didn't bother to follow the thread of the conversation, for Drew's job was as much a mystery to her as hers was to him, merely sat and enjoyed the view.

'I'm sorry,' Joel apologised later as they sat over coffee. 'It was rude to exclude you, but there were certain matters I needed to touch base on with Drew before he leaves.'

Kathryn shrugged that off. She wasn't so vain she needed constant attention. 'No problem. I was far more interested in my food. Agnes is a wonderful cook.'

'I'll be sure to tell her you said so,' he responded, pushing his empty cup away. 'It's not too late. If you're not too tired, we can take a look at the computer now,' he declared with a glance at his watch.

Kathryn was never too tired to work on a computer. 'That's fine by me.' She nodded, and stood up. 'Are you coming, Drew?'

'I'll beg off, if you don't mind. Computers are a complete turn-off for me. Go ahead and enjoy yourselves,' he teased, though, unseen by his cousin, his smile faded as he watched them leave.

Joel's study was at the rear of the house and was set up with state-of-the-art equipment from the computer itself, to fax machines, printers and scanners. Everything he could possibly need was there, but he couldn't use it because of what one woman had done in anger.

'So, this is the scene of the crime,' Kathryn declared dryly, looking around her with interest. 'At least she didn't resort to smashing things. OK, let's see just what damage she did do.' Making herself comfortable at the desk, she switched the computer on, and the first thing that appeared was a message informing Joel he had mail.

'The Internet's working at least,' she observed wryly, hoping it was a good sign that things weren't too bad after all. 'Want to see what it is?'

Standing behind her, his hands resting on the back of her chair, Joel nodded. 'OK.'

Clicking on the box, Kathryn watched the screen unfold. The message itself was short and sweet, and originated from someone called Magda. 'That's her, I take it?' she enquired with lashings of irony, for the message was explicit about what Joel could do with certain parts of his anatomy.

'She has a volatile temper,' Joel said by way of confirmation.

That much was obvious. 'Her knowledge of human anatomy seems a little basic. Does she know you can't actually do that?' she taunted over her shoulder.

'Just get on with it, will you?' he growled irritably, and she bit back a smile. Right now he was more like a grouchy bear than a wolf.

Kathryn started hitting keys. 'I'd get on better if you weren't breathing over my shoulder,' she remarked. It was unsettling, not to say downright distracting. She could feel the heat of his body even through the chair, whilst her nose was assailed by the tangy scent of his cologne mixed with pure male essence. It sent messages to her brain that were totally out of place, even if they were undeniably tantalising.

Instead of moving away, Joel lowered his head until his mouth was next to her ear. 'Does my being this close bother you?' he asked in that sexy drawl which crawled over her flesh, starting up flash-fires which made concentrating on the job at hand extremely difficult.

Feeling too hot and far too bothered for comfort, she nevertheless denied it. 'Not at all.'

'Liar,' he taunted with a chuckle, and she closed her eyes momentarily as a powerful wave of desire swept through her system. She was glad she was sitting, because standing would have been an effort. He was playing hardball, and it didn't help that her senses were fighting on his side.

'Abuse me at your peril,' she warned him, her fingers flying over the keys whilst she struggled to appear cool, calm and collected. It was nothing short of amazing that she never hit a wrong one. 'I can probably do a lot worse to your hard drive than dear Magda did,' she added, then sat back with a tiny frown creasing her forehead.

'How does it look?' Joel asked seriously, and she folded her arms.

'It looks as if she was seriously miffed with you!' Kathryn exclaimed sardonically. From her very brief perusal it was hard to say just how extensive the damage was, but one thing had swiftly become apparent. Magda was no novice when it came to computers. She had known what she was doing.

'We'll take that as read, shall we?' Joel suggested tersely, and Kathryn obligingly subdued her amusement.

'OK, seriously. Have you any idea what's missing?'

'All the work I've been doing on several new projects.'

'Did you keep back-up files on disk?' One look at his face told her the answer to that.

'I made back-up files in the system, but I couldn't find them. I presume she deleted them, too.'

Kathryn sighed heavily. 'In future I suggest you copy sensitive material on disk and put them somewhere safe. At a guess, I'd say all your files are gone. The question is, was she mad enough to wipe them entirely, or did she just trash them? Which means we can retrieve them with a bit of work. Now, if she really wanted to be mean, she could have infected you with a virus.'

'I keep the anti-virus constantly updated,' Joel informed her, and she was relieved, because they could be darned tricky devils.

'Thank goodness for that. Still, I'll check that she didn't set a booby-trap before continuing. You realise there's every probability she wasn't actually physically here, don't you? She would have logged into your database from her own computer. At a guess, I'd say behind her undoubted feminine attractions dear Magda is a dedicated computer hacker,' she declared, looking up to find Joel frowning ferociously.

Catching her eye, he grimaced. 'I had no idea,' he admitted reluctantly.

The confession brought a mocking smile to her lips. 'Yes, well, her brain wasn't what you were interested in, was it?' she pointed out dulcetly.

Give him his due, Joel smiled ruefully, acknowledging the hit. 'We didn't do a lot of talking,' he confirmed, and she shook her head.

'Perhaps you ought to start vetting your women a little more closely. This is the twenty-first century. Women are not merely sex objects any longer. They have brains, and have even been known to use them.'

Straightening, he moved round her and propped a hip against the desk, folding his arms as if prepared to stay there for ever. 'I'm fully aware of that. I employ a good percentage of women in high-profile positions within my organisation.'

He rose a notch in her estimation. 'I'm glad to hear it.'

Joel tutted. 'Can we keep to the point? What I want to know from you is, can you repair the damage?'

Reproved, she folded her hands in her lap. 'Yes, I can. But it's going to take longer than I expected.'

His relief was palpable. 'Take all the time you need. It goes without saying I will pay you whatever you ask. I'm not going to quibble over the bill, because I need those files, and I need them yesterday.'

Kathryn smiled sweetly and pushed up her sleeves. 'Then you'd better let me get on with it. As soon as I've checked that there will be no nasty surprises, I'll be able to move along more quickly. Would you have Drew get my box of tricks for me?' she asked as she reached for the keypad once more.

'I'll get it. What does it look like?'

'It's a small black case. I left it on the dresser in my room,' she responded absently, her mind already running through the checks she would have to make. She didn't hear Joel leave the room, or come back a little later with the case, which he set on the desk beside her.

It was late when she finally closed down the computer and pushed back the chair with a groan as her body protested at having been fixed in one position so long. Yawning, she stretched, easing out the kinks.

'Well, what's the verdict?' A soft voice posed the question from the other side of the room, and she very nearly jumped out of her skin.

Her arms dropped, and, turning startled eyes in the direction the voice had come from, she discovered Joel sitting at his desk, a sheaf of papers in his hand. 'Have you been there all the time?' she charged in amazement, and he nodded.

'Pretty much. I went out for coffee once. Yours will be stone-cold by now,' he told her with some amusement, and Kathryn blinked, only now seeing the cup which had been set at her elbow.

'I didn't hear you,' she confessed, and he laughed softly.

'A herd of elephants could have stampeded through here and you wouldn't have heard them,' he retorted with wry humour.

Her grin was rueful because it was all too possible. 'I do tend to get a little wrapped up in my work.'

'Just a little,' he agreed.

They exchanged smiles, and in the blink of an eye the air seemed to thicken. Kathryn saw the look in his eyes change until its intensity scorched her and her eyes widened, her lips parting on a tiny gasp.

'Are you going to come over here, or am I going to have to come over there?' he asked her in a voice laden with so much passion she shivered.

Her body quickened, her senses silently screaming that either option would do. But there was still a sensible, sane portion of her brain in control, and she shook her head, albeit without any great deal of conviction.

'I think…' she began, only to stop when Joel set his papers down and rose to his feet.

'Don't think,' he ordered huskily, rounding the desk and coming towards her. 'I've been sitting here watching you chew on those luscious lips of yours for the past two hours and it's been driving me crazy,' he added with a groan.

Reaching out, he took her by the shoulders and lifted

her to her feet. Kathryn tried to protest, but her heart wasn't in it. Her hands rose to his chest to hold him off, but that was as far as they got. Instead of pushing him away, her fingers registered the heat of him and spread out like tiny fans to claim all of him they could. Swallowing hard, she stared up at him. Do something, her brain urged, and she did. Her eyelids closed as if weighted and his head descended. When his mouth claimed hers, a wave of such intense pleasure swept through her that her bones seemed to melt. At the brush of his tongue her lips parted, welcoming his possession.

In an instant the world spun away. There was only sensation. Somehow her arms were around his neck, her fingers gliding into silky hair and clinging tightly. From a long way off she heard Joel groan, felt his arms tighten, drawing her to his hard male body, and then his tongue was plundering her mouth with a devastating passion, and she met each thrust with her own, stoking a desire that set her blood sizzling in her veins and started up a throbbing ache deep within her.

It could have been one kiss; it could have been a dozen. Only the need for air finally forced them apart, and they stared at each other, hearts thumping, dragging gasping breaths through kiss-bruised lips.

Joel's eyes had darkened to a deep stormy blue. 'I think I got more than I bargained for,' he confessed thickly.

Kathryn knew that she certainly had. She had always known that this man could make her feel with more intensity than any other man she had ever met, but with that kiss she had entered a whole new realm of experience. Her response had been so quick, so intense, so all-encompassing. Nothing would ever compare to it. Nothing would ever come close.

'You shouldn't have done that.' She made the token protest in a whisper.

'You didn't stop me. You didn't want to,' Joel pointed out unnecessarily, for she knew how foolish she had been. It was too late to take back knowledge. From this point on she would always know what she was missing.

Kathryn pushed herself away from him with very shaky hands. 'Maybe so, but we both know it was a mistake,' she said as forcefully as she was able.

'If that was a mistake, I hope to make more of them,' Joel responded seductively, and the words trickled over her nerve-endings, setting them fluttering.

'Don't,' she protested, then closed her eyes and sighed heavily. 'OK, I admit I enjoyed it. But I'm here to work, not indulge in a…a…a liaison with you!' she continued, with more insistence this time, as her system began to settle down to something approximating normal.

His brows rose quizzically. 'Can't you do both?'

'I don't want to do both!' she lied, and they both knew it.

'Sure you do,' he countered chidingly, and she groaned, realising she was in a hole that would soon be too deep to get herself out of.

'I don't intend to get involved with you, Joel,' she insisted, notwithstanding.

'You can say that when not five minutes ago you went up in flames in my arms?' he charged, and she didn't thank him for reminding her.

Kathryn crossed her arms and raised her chin to a defiant tilt. 'I am saying it.'

Much to her dismay, he merely smiled. 'Now that, in my book, constitutes a challenge. It will give me great satisfaction—and you, too—to make you eat your words.'

Kathryn never had been a woman who knuckled under to attempted male domination—as her brothers could testify. She had a strength of will equal to any man, and if she said no, then no it had to be. 'I wouldn't attempt it if I were you,' she warned frostily, and Joel folded his own arms, mimicking her, and smiled again.

'What will you do to stop me? We've already established that when we get into clinches you fight on my side,' he taunted her, and her eyes narrowed.

'That won't be happening again.'

'You wish!' he shot back with a laugh, and she was very nearly tempted to stamp her foot in frustration. She resisted it, however.

'This is serving no purpose,' she returned, very much on her dignity. 'You do what you feel you have to do, but you won't be getting any co-operation from me.'

'Well, we'll just have to see about that, won't we? Now, why don't you slip off to bed? The rest will do you a power of good,' Joel suggested, and she took umbrage at his tone.

'Don't order me about. I'm not a child.'

The glint in his eye deepened. 'Don't I know it! You're very much a woman, Kathryn Templeton.'

How did he manage to turn the tables on her so easily? 'You are the most... Oh, I'm going to bed!' she exclaimed in frustration, needing to put some space between them so she could regain her equilibrium. 'Goodnight,' she said as she headed for the door.

'Goodnight, Kathryn,' he called after her, and the sound of her name on his lips was a seduction in itself. 'Sweet dreams.'

Her response to that was to close the door firmly

behind her and head for the stairs. She was pretty certain she would dream, but no way would it be sweet. Oh, no. The way things were going, her dreams were more than likely going to be hot and steamy in the extreme. As she mounted the stairs she was very much aware that, for a woman who had no intention of getting involved with a man, the prospect didn't disturb her the way it ought.

CHAPTER THREE

KATHRYN breakfasted alone the following morning, which suited her mood just fine. She had slept, but her dreams had been every bit as erotic as she had suspected they would be. It had been a frustrating night in every sense of the word, and as a consequence she felt less than at her best.

Drew had departed first thing to catch his flight to Germany, and that didn't help cheer her up any, but when Agnes informed her that Joel had insisted on driving him to the airport she breathed a sigh of relief. Putting off the moment of seeing him again seemed like a good idea with a man as perceptive as Joel Kendrick.

She was sipping at a second cup of coffee when she finally heard the car return, and instinctively braced herself. He came in not long afterwards, and, as before, she felt his presence like a charge in the air. She didn't turn around, though, and therefore jumped like a scalded cat when his hands descended on her shoulders and he bent to press a tingling kiss to the tender skin of her neck just below her ear.

'Good morning, Kathryn,' he greeted warmly, and released her before she could have the satisfaction of pulling away.

Annoyed that she hadn't anticipated the manoeuvre, she glowered at him as he poured himself some coffee, then pulled out the chair opposite her and sat down.

'Good morning,' she returned frostily, and his brows shot up above dancing eyes.

'Didn't you sleep well?' he asked, sounding concerned, but she knew that wasn't what he was thinking at all. He knew. Don't ask her how, but he knew.

'I never sleep well in strange beds,' she countered, not giving him the satisfaction of confirming that dreaming of him had made her so restless. 'But as it's only for two nights, I think I'll survive it.'

'Actually, it could turn out to be more. There's a weather front moving in, and they're promising us strong winds and some serious snowfall,' Joel enlightened her, resting his elbows on the table and sipping his coffee as if he hadn't a care in the world and hadn't just dropped a potential bombshell. Kathryn frowned sharply.

'What does that mean, exactly?' Surely she would be able to leave tomorrow? She had to. She was counting on it, she thought, a shade too desperately for comfort.

Joel disabused her in no uncertain terms. 'It means we could wake tomorrow to find ourselves snowed in for the duration. Something we've become used to up here.'

'You're not serious!' Kathryn gasped in dismay, only to see him nod.

'It was already beginning to snow as I drove home. But don't worry. If it does happen, you'll be perfectly safe here.'

Kathryn was not comforted. The definition of 'safe' depended on your point of view. It would not be safe being snowed in here with him, yet she couldn't leave until she had done the work she had promised. Whichever way you looked at it, she was trapped. She just had to hope and pray the snow held off long enough for her to get the work done and leave on time.

She sipped at her coffee, her free hand absently rubbing over the spot his lips had touched. Her skin still tingled with the charge which had ripped along her nervous system. It was incredibly stimulating, but it wasn't going to change her mind. She wouldn't get involved with him. Sighing, she glanced up, right into a pair of twinkling blue eyes.

'Incredible, isn't it?' Joel remarked as she jerked her hand away. 'I found it difficult to sleep last night myself, and I'm used to sleeping here. I kept remembering how it felt to have you in my arms. I wanted to feel it again. I had this fantasy of seeing you in my bed, your glorious hair spread out around you like a halo. It was incredibly erotic,' he added with husky sensuality, and with no effort at all Kathryn could imagine it, too.

Her body responded without conscious volition, her nipples hardening into highly sensitive nubs that cried out to be touched. The hardest part was knowing that she could have that, just for walking round the table and going to him. Making love with him would be an experience never to be forgotten. Yet, though she might remember it always, she doubted very much that he would. She would soon be replaced, and it was that knowledge which kept her in her seat.

'So, you believe in fantasies but not fairy tales?' she retorted, in an effort to alter the course of the conversation.

His smile acknowledged her hit. 'With a subtle difference. You can make your fantasies come true, but fairy stories will always be pure fiction.'

'Are you scared of commitment? Is that what it is?' she couldn't help asking curiously, but Joel shook his head.

'If and when I marry, the relationship will have my

full commitment, but I won't be dressing it up in the gloss of love and romance.'

'So you do intend to get married?' Kathryn asked at his unexpected response. She had imagined him as a confirmed bachelor.

'Of course. It is possible to have a good marriage based on mutual respect, Kathryn. People do it all the time.'

Which was true enough, but it sounded so…cold. Physical passion, however strong, could never replace love. True love survived long after passion was spent.

'I suppose so,' she agreed reluctantly. 'It just wouldn't be enough for me. But as it's a subject we are hardly likely ever to agree on, I'll take myself off to the study. There's a lot of work to do, and I want to get as much done as I can today,' she declared, setting her cup down and rising to her feet.

'I'll be along shortly,' Joel responded, which wasn't at all what she wanted.

'There's no need,' she countered hastily. 'If there's anything I need to talk to you about, I can come and find you.' The last thing she needed was to be shut up in the same room with him all day.

Joel smiled faintly, as if he guessed her reasoning. 'I'm sure you would, but I happen to have some work to do myself. I might as well get on with it, and at least I'll be on hand should the need arise,' he added sardonically, and she knew she was beaten.

'I'll see you in a bit, then,' she managed to say graciously, before quickly leaving the room.

Damn, she thought to herself, she didn't need this. Yet there was nothing she could do about it. It was his house and his study. She could hardly forbid him entry, however much she would have liked to. She would just have to grin and bear it.

Once in Joel's study, she made herself comfortable at the keypad and was quickly engrossed in her work. Retrieving the files was simple enough, but it was time-consuming. Fortunately the deleted files were dated, so it was easy enough to know which were the relevant files, and which had been Joel's intentional deletions. By midday, everything with a corresponding date was back in the main system.

With a feeling of satisfaction, Kathryn turned to where Joel sat at his desk, studying a batch of papers. She had been aware of his presence ever since he had come in, but he had said nothing to her, merely crossed to his desk and got down to business. Which had been a great relief. Now, though, she had to gain his attention.

As if sensing her gaze, Joel glanced up, one eyebrow lifting in silent query.

'I've retrieved everything for the date you think Magda got into the system. You'd better come and check if it's all there,' she invited, and Joel immediately rose to his feet and came to join her.

She had expected him to sit, but he chose to read the screen over her shoulder, one hand resting on the desk, taking his weight as he leaned closer. Kathryn was made very much aware of him. The musky scent of him assailed her nostrils, affording her senses a subtle pleasure.

'Let me just...' Joel began, reaching round her to take the mouse, and suddenly Kathryn found herself trapped between both his arms, with his torso pressing against her head and shoulders. Her breathing grew ragged as her heart slipped into a higher gear. She had an almost overwhelming urge to lean back against him and have those strong male arms enfold her. She might even have done it, except that the tone of Joel's voice altered, bringing her back to sanity.

'That's odd,' he murmured shortly, and she could tell from his tone that he was frowning.

She sat up straighter immediately, pushing all wanton thought aside. 'What is?'

'The files I've been working on aren't there,' he told her, and she frowned, too.

'Are you sure? What name are they under?' Joel told her and she took the mouse from him and started clicking. It only took a minute or two to confirm he was right. Those files were missing. 'I'll go back over my tracks. Perhaps she got in more than once, and those files have a different date. Give me some time to check it out.' Without waiting for his agreement, Kathryn started to hunt down the missing files.

Half an hour later she sat back with a grim expression on her face. Folding her arms, she turned to where Joel stood waiting by the window. He looked round at once, his shoulders tensing as he saw the serious set of her mouth.

'They're not there,' he stated shortly, and she nodded.

'They're gone, all right. Was the information on them vital?' It wasn't mere curiosity. She needed to know in order to think of what to do next.

Joel dragged a hand through his hair. 'They were highly confidential, concerning some new projects I'm working on. I used them all the time. She probably guessed that the files I used most often were current and wiped them totally,' he said in a voice that threatened retribution if he ever met up with the lady again.

Kathryn shivered. She wouldn't want to make an enemy of him. Unfortunately, what she had to say next wouldn't improve his mood, either. 'There is another possibility, and only you will know if it's feasible,' she ventured, and his eyes narrowed.

'And that is?'

Looking him squarely in the eye, because she had discovered it was better to deliver bad news without dressing it up, she gave him her worst case scenario. 'She may have copied the files onto disks, then deleted them permanently to make you think just what you have,' she said, and caught her breath when he seemed to freeze, a stunned look crossing his face.

'The devil!' he exclaimed through gritted teeth, and she could see his brain suddenly working like fury to follow that line of reasoning to its conclusion.

'It's possible, then?'

'More than possible,' Joel agreed wrathfully, and she winced.

Kathryn watched him, unblinking, then gave a tiny cough before posing her next question cautiously. 'Er...just how well did you know Magda? I hate to be the ghost at the feast, but was this an act of pure serendipity, or did she get to know you as part of another agenda, to get the information on your projects?' she asked, and could swear she heard his teeth grinding.

'I'm just beginning to wonder that myself,' he returned grimly, dragging his hand through his hair again as he paced back and forth across the room. Finally he came to a halt before her. 'OK, get your coat on. We're going for a walk. I need to think and I need fresh air to do it.'

Though she raised her brows in surprise, Kathryn didn't argue. The man had problems, and right now he didn't need her adding to them. Perhaps she might even be able to help. Without a word she quickly shut the computer down and hurried upstairs to change into jeans and a thick sweater. Tugging on her boots, she gathered up her coat and went down to find him pacing the hall impatiently. He had donned a thick, fleece-lined coat, pulled a woollen hat onto his head and wound a scarf around his neck. When he saw her slipping into her woollen coat, he tutted and strode to the closet, returning with several items in his hands.

'You'll freeze in just that coat,' he declared tersely, and proceeded to pull a cream woolly hat onto her head and, before she could protest, wound a matching scarf round her neck.

Feeling very much like a small child being dressed for the outdoors by an adult, Kathryn couldn't help grinning as she swayed back and forth under his ministrations. When he noticed it, he stood back and frowned.

'What's so funny?' he asked, and she giggled.

'I was just imagining you doing this to your own child. I bet you'd make a good father,' she pronounced just a little huskily.

Still frowning, Joel began pulling on a pair of gloves. 'You decided that on the basis of my putting a hat and scarf on you?'

Kathryn nodded. 'Because despite you being angry and upset, and having a million more important things to think about, you were still concerned about my well-being. It's called caring, in case you don't recognise it,' she added ironically, and he shot her a darkling look.

'Don't read anything into it. I just don't want you getting sick on me. Do you have gloves? Put them on then,' he ordered when she produced them from her pockets, magician fashion.

'Yes, Papa,' she returned demurely, and this time

when he looked at her his mood had lightened slightly, enough for a faint glimmer of amusement to appear in his eyes.

'Cut it out, or I'll do another fatherly thing and box your ears for you!'

Ducking her head to hide another grin, Kathryn subsided obediently and meekly followed him out of the front door. The cold hit her immediately, and she was instantly glad of the hat and scarf. It was snowing only fitfully at present, but the wind had picked up considerably, and she could well imagine that they were soon going to get the promised snowstorm.

Joel set out at a brisk pace down the hillside towards the lake. Kathryn had to hurry to keep up with him, but she made no complaint, for he was already deep in thought again. She could barely imagine what he must be thinking, but she knew it would not be pleasant. The ramifications of their suspicions were enough to set her own stomach churning. If someone had broken into her computer and stolen files, she knew she wouldn't just mourn their loss, she would feel violated, too, for a computer was a very personal thing. Right now Joel must be feeling betrayed. It was no wonder he had some serious thinking to do.

Which was why she said nothing when she began to struggle with the pace, merely put her head down and battled to keep up with him as he followed a barely visible path through the trees to the lake shore. There, without warning, he stopped. The move was so sudden she had no time to avoid him and careened into his back.

'Oh! Ouch! Sorry,' she apologised as she bounced off him and stumbled backwards.

One long arm snaked out and grabbed her before she

fell, steadying her. He noted the way her chest was heaving with her effort to keep pace with him, and frowned.

'You're out of shape.'

The comment, when she had been doing her best to be reasonable, stung, and she brushed his hand away. 'I'm in fine shape, thank you very much. You should have warned me we were in a race. Funnily enough, I assumed a walk meant just that!' she returned indignantly, and he had the grace to look a little shamefaced.

'Sorry,' he apologised in turn. 'I forgot you were there.'

Oh, this just got better and better! 'What an insult! You order my presence like some olde worlde potentate, after which I become instantly forgettable!' she gibed, and was a little surprised at how relieved she was to see him smile, however faintly.

'Now, that you could never be,' he said, then shook his head. 'Would you have kept on at the same pace until you collapsed from exhaustion?'

Her shoulders rose and fell. 'Like a faithful hound. I was banking on you being sorry when you realised what you'd done. I pictured you bent over my unconscious body, damning your selfishness.'

At that he shot her an old-fashioned look. 'Why didn't you just tell me I was walking too fast, hmm?'

She waved a hand airily. 'I wasn't really worried. I knew I'd get my second wind. By the way, I think I should point out that you'll never outrun the problem. But, if you're determined to walk your legs down to stumps, I'll keep you company.'

He gave her a strange look then, as if he didn't quite know what to make of her. 'The faithful hound?'

Kathryn smiled up at him. 'Something like that. Is

the air fresh enough for you to think clearly?' It felt
cold enough to her to do physical damage to metal mon-
keys.

Joel glanced about him and took a deep lungful. 'It's
certainly brisk,' he admitted, tongue-in-cheek. 'We'd
better get moving or there's every possibility we'll
freeze on the spot.'

No kidding, she thought wryly.

This time they set off at a more reasonable pace,
which caused her no problems. Joel soon plunged back
into thought, and Kathryn left him to it. She knew he
would speak when he had something to say. For herself,
now that she had caught her breath, she had ample opportunity to study the stark beauty of the lake in winter.
It could have been alienating, but to her it had a kind
of magical quality. In a frosty, mystical landscape like
this it was easy to imagine oneself lost in the deep
reaches of Middle Earth.

She was busy visualising conflicts of good and evil
swaying back and forth over the lake when Joel's footsteps began to slow, and with a shake of her head she
returned to the present. Crunch time. Turning to face
the water, he shoved his hands into his pockets and
stared out across the chilly expanse. Kathryn found a
conveniently tumbled log, brushed off the snow and
made herself comfortable on it, her gaze locked on his
back as she waited. It wasn't long before Joel spoke.

'This is something I should have been expecting, but
the last incident was so long ago I got sloppy. I failed
to see it coming,' he explained, convolutedly, and her
brows rose.

'You expected this?' she asked in surprise.

'Not this specifically, but something like it. Before
we get to that, I'd better explain Magda's involvement.

I met her about a month ago. She backed her car into mine. At the time I suspected it was a deliberate accident to catch my attention, but that isn't unusual,' he revealed with a heavy dose of self-mockery.

Kathryn could easily picture the scene. Blonde beauty in severe distress over the shunt. Strong handsome type offers comfort, tells her not to worry her pretty little head about it, and…meeting achieved. 'Now you don't think it was that innocent?'

With a growl of disgust, Joel turned and looked at her. 'Not considering the timing. I'd forgotten, but now I realise we're coming up to the anniversary. This isn't about business at all. It's about one man getting revenge on another.'

'Revenge for what, exactly?' she queried carefully. The plot had thickened and she felt all at sea. Joel sighed heavily.

'For something I did wrong a long time ago. Gray, the man I believe is behind this, used to be my best friend, until I walked off with his girlfriend. What I didn't know was that he was in love with her. What he didn't know was that she threw herself at me, and, being stupid, I caught her instead of throwing her back. The long and the short of it is, she was out for what she could get. But it was no use my trying to tell him that. He refused to listen. All he knew was that I had stolen the woman he loved. Ever since then he's been doing his best to score points off me in whatever way he can. This little stunt is just the sort of thing he would do. I'd be willing to bet that somehow he persuaded Magda to do it for him.'

This had all the makings of an off-off-Broadway stage play. 'I see. The chickens have come home to roost with a vengeance this time. The big question is, can he make use of what's on the files?' She homed in on the important point, but Joel swiftly shook his head.

He came to sit beside her and propped his elbows on his knees. This close, Kathryn could see his breath freezing in the air as he spoke. 'No. We're not in the same line of business. My guess is Magda took the files because they were what I was working on, not because of what they contained. Gray will know the importance if he reads them.'

'And what will he do with them?'

Joel ran a hand around his neck tiredly. 'I have no idea. But I wouldn't put it past him to hold them over my head until he has exacted what he considers a fitting revenge.'

'Hmm, looks like he has you over a barrel. If you do whatever he asks, will he return the files?'

'I believe so. He just wants to make me suffer for a while,' Joel explained grimly. 'I have to hand it to him; he was clever. He knew me so well, he chose the one way of getting someone into my home without making me suspect anything.'

Kathryn shuffled her feet, which were beginning to feel the cold, and wisely chose not to comment. 'What are you going to do?' It didn't seem to her that allowing this man called Gray to get away with it was Joel's way, and he confirmed it in the next minute.

'Get the files back, of course,' he said grittily, and his strength of purpose was underlined by the hard set of his jaw.

Her brows rose. 'Fine words, but just how do you intend to go about it?' she asked curiously, and he turned those piercing blue eyes on her, capturing her gaze.

'*I'm* not going to do anything. *You* are,' he said

softly, taking her aback. The steadiness of his regard sent her a clear message, and her eyes rounded into saucers.

'You're not seriously suggesting...?' The remainder of the sentence tailed off into nothingness. Her teeth snapped together and she sat up straighter. 'I can't do that!'

He sat up, too. 'Of course you can. You told me you were better than Magda. What she did, you can do in reverse,' he argued firmly, and her eyes narrowed as he totally missed her point.

'I'm not saying I *can't* do it, I mean I *won't* do it,' she refused bluntly. Maybe in her early days at university she had enjoyed the thrill of hacking into different systems, but those days were long gone. She was a respectable businesswoman now. 'It's not ethical.'

'Ethics be damned!' Joel countered explosively. 'I'm not asking you to break into the system of a rival in order to steal. All I'm asking is for you to do what has been done to me. This isn't going to end up in court with your reputation in shreds. This is private, between the two of us, and will go no further whatever happens. Now, I believe we have time on our side. I'm betting Gray doesn't expect me to link it to him—at least not yet. So far as he knows, his tracks are still covered. Ordinarily I would be prepared to let Gray get away with it, but not in this case. I need those files back, and you're the only person who can get them for me.'

'Rubbish! There's any number of people out there who would be only too happy to do it for you,' Kathryn insisted, but Joel was having none of it. He caught her by the shoulders and forced her to face him.

'Maybe there are, but they aren't here and you are. You have to help me, Kathryn. Please. I need you.'

She'd been about to refuse yet again. Those three simple words kept her silent. Her heart seemed to give a crazy lurch and she bit her lip. Oh, damn. He had had to put it like that, hadn't he? He needed her help. He had even said please! How could she refuse him? She worried her lip some more, and caught the faint sound of a stifled groan. She blinked, and discovered that Joel's eyes were no longer looking at her own, but had dropped to her mouth and were locked there in fatal fascination.

'Do you have any idea what it does to me when you do that?' he asked in a low growl that set the fine hairs on her flesh rising.

Kathryn was very much aware that though her extremities were feeling the cold, parts of her were definitely warming up. 'You don't have to try and persuade me. I've already decided to help you, though it goes against the grain,' she admitted, finding it incredibly difficult to speak when he was looking at her like that.

A faint smile curled the edges of his lips and made her knees melt, so that she couldn't have moved away if she wanted to. 'Then I think I should thank you properly,' he declared thickly, drawing her towards him as he angled his head, the better to take her mouth.

In the back of her mind sanity urged she put up a fight, but Kathryn wasn't listening. Forgetting everything she had told herself not to do, she sighed and shivered with pleasure when his lips claimed hers, but it was a fleeting caress that was over much too soon. In dismay she blinked at him when he pulled back.

'Thank you, Kathryn,' he murmured softly, a dangerous light glimmering in the depths of his eyes.

'Is that it?' she asked, unable to hide her disappointment, then caught the tiny flash of triumph in those incredible blue orbs and knew that she had been successfully reeled in. 'Oh, you rat!' she exclaimed, and would have fought him then. He defeated her by the simple act of taking her mouth again.

Only this time it was completely different. He captured her lips with a passion that stole her breath away, and as she gasped he growled, and his tongue claimed her honeyed sweetness, plundering it remorselessly. Swept away on a tide of pleasure, she let her arms slide up around his neck and his arms enfolded her, drawing her as close as their bulky clothing would allow. In seconds they were lost to the world, exchanging kisses that aroused and tantalised, building a fire that threatened to rage out of control.

It was Joel who finally dragged his mouth away. Struggling for breath, he rested his forehead against hers, their frozen breaths mingling like wraiths around them.

'You must be some kind of witch,' he panted. 'There's a kind of magic in those lips of yours that make me want to keep coming back for more.' Framing her face with his gloved hands, he eased her head back so that he could look into her eyes. 'We're sitting on a log, with the snow falling around us, and I can barely keep my hands off you! I've got to be crazy!'

When it came to craziness, that made two of them. What was she thinking of? Why was it that every time he touched her every sane and sensible thought vanished? Who had put a spell on who? The question sent a wave of unease through her, and she couldn't say why. What she did know was that the breathing space had given her sanity the opportunity to recover. She placed her hands over his and prised them away.

'You have some pretty potent magic of your own,

but I guess you've had enough practice to get it down to a fine art,' she said dryly, wishing her pulse would settle down.

Joel dropped his hands and gave her a look of wry amusement. 'Ouch. You certainly know how to hit below the belt. I meant what I said, Kathryn. There's something extra special about you,' he insisted, and Kathryn sighed.

'I'm sure you mean it every time you say it.'

He frowned at her. Watching her get to her feet. 'That wasn't a very nice thing to say.'

She shoved her hands into her coat pockets and stamped her feet to get some feeling back into them. 'It isn't very nice to know you're just the latest in a long line.'

Joel got up too, and stood staring down at her with a faint frown still between his eyes. 'That is something I can do nothing about.'

'I know. Your past is a matter of public—very public—record. I'd rather avoid being just another statistic. It's a female thing. You wouldn't understand,' she told him mockingly.

'You're wrong; I do understand. You've always been different from the rest, that's why I find you so fascinating. I've never come across anyone quite like you before,' Joel countered. 'As to your being a statistic… You know I would never force you into anything, but I reserve the right to try and persuade you to change your mind.'

Kathryn didn't even have to think about it. She knew instinctively that Joel would never take what was not freely given. It was up to her to remain firm. The trouble with that was that he was so damned persuasive.

'Personally, I think I'm doing enough by agreeing to

track down those files of yours,' she returned dryly, and his expression became serious.

'It would be a debt I could never fully repay, and I wouldn't ask you to do it if it wasn't vitally important. The new projects are something my company could live without, but to allow this to happen once without doing something would be to invite it again. That I am not prepared to accept.'

Kathryn shook her head wonderingly. 'You know, for an unprincipled rogue, you have a surprising number of principles.'

At that he grinned. 'Even a rogue has his limits. Speaking of which, I've just reached my tolerance level for cold. The snow's getting heavier by the minute. It would be madness to stay here any longer. Let's go home.'

It was a suggestion she was happy to fall in with, for the weather was deteriorating drastically. In a reversal of roles, she was the one looked in thought on the way back, and it was all due to her companion. Like the best-laid schemes, hers was going wrong. Resisting Joel, she was beginning to realise, was going to be easier said than done.

CHAPTER FOUR

KATHRYN stirred and rolled onto her back with a sigh. As she lay there, wriggling her toes in the comfort of the duvet, she slowly became aware of the silence, and raised herself on her elbows, looking towards the window. Last night a blizzard had been howling around the house, making her start at every sudden bang and crash. Now it had stopped, leaving an almost eerie quietness. Throwing back the duvet, she climbed from the bed and went to the window, pulling aside the curtains only to gasp at the sight which met her eyes.

The whole world was white for as far as the eye could see. Thick drifts of snow lay everywhere, several feet deep, and it was still snowing with those thick flakes that said it had been doing so for some hours and had no intention of stopping any time soon. As Joel had predicted, they were snowed in.

She shivered, though the room was cosy and warm, due to the central heating. Kathryn had learned from Agnes that Joel had fires lit in some rooms because he preferred them to radiators. Thinking of Agnes only served to remind her that the other woman was no longer in the house, nor likely to be for the next few days, given the conditions. Apparently she always spent Saturday evening and Sunday in Kendal with friends, and as soon as they had returned from their walk Joel had insisted she go early, before it became hazardous to drive. After protesting, she had given in to his urging, and consequently Kathryn and Joel were alone in the house.

It was not an ideal situation, but Kathryn was determined to play it cool. So she had to stay here for a few extra days. That didn't mean anything was going to happen. Last night they had eaten the dinner Agnes had prepared for them and then spent the evening together quite comfortably, listening to the radio and talking. In fact, she couldn't remember when she had enjoyed an evening more. They had chatted about surprisingly disparate subjects, finding they had many things in common.

Leaning against the window frame, she allowed a tiny smile to tug at the corners of her mouth as she ran through the evening in her mind. She remembered being enthralled yet again by the animation on his face as he'd talked about his favourite subject. She wondered if he was aware that he laughed with his eyes when something really amused him. He wasn't at all the kind of man she had expected from his reputation. He had been relaxed and at ease, and the attempted seduction that Drew would have expected had never materialised.

In fact, she had enjoyed herself so much she had been loath to go to bed. It had only been when she'd found it impossible to stifle a jaw-breaking yawn that she had reluctantly taken herself off to her room. There she had tumbled into bed and been asleep almost as soon as her head had touched the pillow. Now it was morning, and she could feel an unexpected bubble of anticipation inside her. Crazy as it might sound, she was actually looking forward to seeing him again.

Which had to be the craziest feeling she had ever had, she berated herself as she pushed herself upright and reached for the robe that matched her long cream silk nightdress. It was early yet: not quite seven, according to her watch. She would just pop down to the kitchen and make herself some coffee. She would need the kick-start if she seriously intended to solve the matter of tracking down the missing files.

Barefoot, she padded quietly down the stairs and along the hall to the kitchen. Pushing the door open, she was brought up short with a gasp of surprise when she found the room already occupied. Joel stood at the counter, idly stirring a mug of coffee as he stared out at the snow. He turned at the sound of her entrance, the spoon slowing to a stop, and there was an arrested look on his face when he saw her standing there.

He was barefoot, too...and bare-legged. In fact she was pretty sure the towelling robe he wore, which gaped above the belt, allowing her a glimpse of silky dark chest hair, was the only thing he wore. It was a mind-blowing thought, and she suddenly found herself fighting an urge to go to him and discover for herself if that hair was as silky as it looked. Joel meanwhile allowed his eyes to travel the length of her and back again. It was like a caress, and Kathryn felt her body tighten in response.

Oh, God, she thought faintly. It was barely seven o'clock in the morning and the room was alive with that peculiar electricity they always generated whenever they came close to each other.

Joel cleared his throat. 'That has to be the sexiest number I've ever seen,' he declared gruffly, and the sound made her senses leap.

She laughed edgily. 'It covers me from top to toe,' she pointed out unnecessarily, and he grinned that wolf-ish grin which engendered various emotions in her, none of which was fear.

'I know. It's making my imagination work overtime in ways you can't imagine.'

Oh, Kathryn wasn't so sure about that. She could imagine all too clearly what he was thinking, and it didn't help to ease the curling sensation inside her.

'Are you coming or going?' Joel asked before she could form a rational response, and she wasn't too sure about that either. It was the effect he seemed to have on her.

'Ask me an easier one,' she quipped back wryly, knowing she was giving a lot away, but doubting that he had been unaware of it anyway.

In response, a gleam entered his eyes, and, abandoning his coffee, he prowled across the floor towards her. She tensed automatically, but all he did was take her hand and pull her a step or two into the room so that he could push the door closed behind her. Then, smiling faintly, he took a step closer and Kathryn backed up— only to meet the solid wood of the door. She was trapped, and they both knew it.

Joel placed his palms flat against the door, either side of her head, and his eyes glittered. 'Now what are you going to do?' he taunted softly.

Wise or not, Kathryn had never been one to back down from a challenge. Instead of doing the obvious thing, and demanding he let her go, she did what she had been secretly longing to do anyway. She reached up and slipped her hand inside the lapel of his robe and ran her palm caressingly over the taut skin of his chest. It was music to her ears to hear his breath hiss through his teeth as she took him by surprise, and her pulse-rate soared skywards.

'How was that for starters?' she goaded naughtily, and would have made good her escape by ducking under his arm. But he was one step ahead of her and foiled her by the simple act of taking that half-step which brought his body into full contact with hers. This time it was her breath that caught in her throat as she clearly felt the evidence of his arousal.

'Oh, no, you don't!' he said quickly. 'You don't get away with it that easily.'

Kathryn tipped her head up, eyes glittering with defiance and something far more potent. 'You started it,' she accused. It was impossible for her to move, with one hand trapped between their two bodies. Not that she really wanted to. Her senses were going crazy with the scent and feel of him. Beneath her hand she could feel the rhythmic thud of his racing heart, and it matched her own.

Joel's hands cupped her face, his fingers tangling in her hair. 'And I'm about to finish it,' he murmured sexily. 'You shouldn't have done that.'

'You shouldn't have dared me,' she shot back faintly, all the strength seeming to go out of her voice as her eyes locked on his mouth, so tantalisingly close to her own. Lord, how she wanted to feel it on her own, creating the magic that only he could conjure up.

'If you keep looking at me like that, I'm going to have to kiss you.' Joel issued the warning from low in his throat, and she raised heavy-lidded eyes to his.

'What's stopping you?' she whispered through a painfully tight throat, and he laughed softly.

'Damned if I know,' he admitted, and finally brought his mouth down on hers.

Her sigh of pleasure was lost as her lips parted to the insistent caress of his tongue. Her free hand clutched at the cloth on his back, holding on as their kisses stoked fires still smouldering from the last time. They went up like dry tinder, Joel's hands leaving her face to seek out the silk-covered curves of her back. She shivered with delight as his hands fastened on her hips and pulled her closer. Pressing herself against him, she struggled to free her other hand and slip it around his neck. At the same time she felt his hands gliding upwards, finding her waist, then his thumbs discovered the swell of her breasts and she stopped thinking. Her body surged, her breasts waiting achingly for his touch, and when it came she moaned at the exquisite pleasure. Joel's response was to press her back against the door and slip one powerful thigh between hers.

The jarring tones of the telephone broke them apart with all the finesse of a bucket of cold water, and it took them a moment to realise just what it was. Cursing under his breath, Joel dragged a hand through his hair and stalked to the phone which hung on the wall, barely managing to speak civilly.

Kathryn closed her eyes and pressed a hand to her bruised lips. This was all getting out of hand. She was supposed to be doing the sensible thing, not encouraging him. But when he got close things always got jumbled in her mind—when she was able to think at all. What on earth was the matter with her? Why couldn't she simply keep some distance between them?

She heard Joel replace the receiver and opened her eyes again. He was looking at her through smouldering eyes as he came back to her. Reaching out, he ran his hands slowly up and down her upper arms.

'That was my neighbour. He was checking up on us. I told him we were OK for food and heating. He uses his tractor to help clear the roads for the outlying houses. If the snow stops today, he'll be out to clear the lane. If not, it will be tomorrow at the earliest,' he explained concisely, then his eyes lowered to her mouth broodingly. 'Now, where were we…?' He made a move to close the distance between them, and Kathryn raised her hands quickly to keep him at bay.

'Oh, no. I don't think so,' she refused, having had time to cool her heated blood.

'Before Wilf rang you were more than ready to be swept upstairs to my bed,' Joel argued persuasively, and she couldn't deny it.

'Your friend has impeccable timing,' she returned calmly, although she was still far from calm on the inside.

'You mean he gave you time to change your mind,' Joel responded ironically, and to give him his due, however frustrated he was, he was far from being angry.

'It is a woman's privilege,' Kathryn added softly, fully aware that her behaviour had given him every reason to suppose she intended going to bed with him. Which she probably would have done, had the phone not rung. 'I'm sorry.'

Joel released her and stepped away. 'Don't be. I won't pretend I'm not disappointed, but there will be other times, and, as I told you before, I would never force a woman.' Turning round, he went back to where his mug of coffee stood cooling on the countertop. Lifting the coffee pot, he glanced at her over his shoulder. 'Coffee?'

'Thanks.' She nodded, attempting to pull herself together, when in truth all of her senses were still vitally aware of him. 'I guess you're what my mother would call a true gentleman. I, on the other hand, wasn't very ladylike. I shouldn't have taken that dare,' she added wryly as she crossed the room.

Turning, he held out a mug. 'Take my word for it,

Kathryn, when it comes to being a lady, you're hell on wheels. Which is why I will probably spend the next hour taking cold showers,' he observed with wry humour, smiling into her eyes, and it was in that instant, when she looked into those blue depths as she was taking the mug from him, that she made a startling discovery.

She had fallen in love with him.

It was the sort of revelation that made everything she had been feeling that much clearer, and, conversely, at the same time made everything unbelievably complicated. For there was nothing simple in falling for Joel Kendrick, except the manner of it. She had looked into his eyes and been lost. It was clear to her now that since the very first she had been fighting a losing battle. Unbeknownst to her, love had hit her like a bolt of lightning. Whilst she had thought herself flirting with a powerful attraction, deep in her heart had been hidden the fact that, as she had always expected it would be, she had fallen in love with him on sight.

'Is everything OK?' Joel's concerned voice broke into her jumbled thoughts and brought her back to the present.

Nerves jangling for quite another reason now, she stepped back from him, automatically cradling the mug for comfort. 'Everything's fine,' she insisted just a fraction too hastily, and caught his frown. 'I'm fine, really. Something just occurred to me, that's all,' she added, and that had to be the understatement to end all understatements.

'About the missing files?' he asked at once, and she quickly set his mind at rest.

'Oh, no. It was personal. Nothing to do with work at all.'

'Is it something you want to talk about?' he probed, taking his own mug and following her to the table, and her laugh carried the faintest edge of hysteria. This was the very last thing she would ever discuss with him.

'Not right now. It was nothing, really.' She refused his offer, and grimaced at the lie. Nothing? It was everything.

Sitting facing her, he didn't look convinced. 'You looked as if you'd seen a ghost,' he remarked, and that seemed very apt to Kathryn.

In a way she had seen a ghost. The ghost of all her hopes and dreams. She had always taken it for granted that the man she fell in love with would feel the same about her. Now she realised how naive she had been. It was entirely possible to fall for someone who didn't love you. Someone who would never love you, because he didn't believe in love in the first place.

Kathryn tucked a stray strand of hair behind her ear with fingers that carried a faint tremor and smiled crookedly. 'No. No ghost. You might say an unpalatable truth just reared up and bit me.' She attempted to make light of it, for one thing was patently clear: she mustn't ever let him know that she had fallen for him. Her wound might be self-inflicted, but it was her wound, and if she couldn't have his love, she certainly didn't want his pity.

Joel looked sympathetic. 'Truths have a habit of doing that,' he agreed wryly.

Didn't they just? Sighing, Kathryn took another sip of coffee. 'This weekend isn't turning out at all the way I expected,' she said with a wry shake of her head.

'What were you expecting?'

She laughed softly, though it was directed mostly at

herself. 'I certainly wasn't expecting you. You came as quite a surprise,' she declared honestly.

His smile was full of self-mockery. 'I wasn't prepared for you, either. Women don't usually go toe to toe with me.'

She quirked an eyebrow at him, not doubting it in the least. 'The way they apparently keep falling at your feet, you must be tripping over them all the time.'

Blue eyes glittered appreciatively. 'It can certainly be a hazard to my health. I have to do some fancy footwork to avoid them.'

It was amazing how heavy those light words hung in her heart. 'Do you avoid many?' she asked, with the scepticism he expected of her, and Joel shook his head reprovingly.

'If I'd had all the women I'm reputed to have had, I'd be a physical wreck by now.'

She forced herself to grin, amazed at how easy it was to keep up the appearance of insouciance. Which was as well, for it was necessary on her part. 'I'm happy to say you're in good physical condition.'

That had his eyes narrowing. 'I'm glad you like my body, because I'm rather partial to yours, too.'

Kathryn's heart flinched at the statement, which showed just how divergent their feelings were. His desire might be honest, but it hurt unbearably, and she struggled not to let it show. Her only defence was to be the light-hearted woman he expected. 'Have you always been this incorrigible?' she teased.

His teeth gleamed as his smile broadened. 'According to my mother, I was a perfect little angel, but then, she is biased.'

'Which means she knows you have more than a little bit of the devil in you.'

'If I hadn't, you wouldn't be attracted to me,' he pointed out roguishly, and she met the challenge honestly.

'True. I never did go much for angels. Who would choose a saint, when a sinner could be much more fun?' she returned with false brightness.

'So when are you going to go to bed with me and find out just how much "fun" I can be?' Joel charged outrageously, and Kathryn's nerves jumped as if they had touched a live wire.

'Oh, this year. Next year. Some time. Never...' Her throat closed over, and when she spoke the last word of the rhyme her voice was painfully husky.

A frown creased her brow, and her eyes dropped to her mug, although she barely registered it. It had hit her, with the childish rhyme she had begun so airily, that never was a long, long time. Opportunities were fleeting. These few days could be the only time she would ever have with Joel out of a whole lifetime. It was a prospect that made her feel so very, very cold inside. Their relationship had changed and so must her response to it. It was no longer a simple question of whether a brief affair would damage her self-respect or not. He had become more to her than that, and, consequently, this time had suddenly become precious.

'Kathryn?' Joel's hand touched hers, and she looked up with a start. 'You were miles away, and it didn't seem a very nice place to be,' he explained gently, with unexpected seriousness.

His touch was like a brand searing into her soul, and she eased her hand out from under his, because right now it hurt too much. 'I was just thinking how fleeting time was. Which isn't like me at all. It must be all this white silence. It's giving me the creeps,' she lied, covering her emotionalism with an exaggerated shudder.

'They call it cabin fever, but I imagine it takes longer than twelve hours to set in. For most people it should take days, if not weeks,' Joel observed ironically, and she smiled faintly.

'Well, that only goes to show I'm not like most people,' Kathryn riposted neatly, and saw those banked fires in his eyes set off a few sparks at her words.

'You certainly aren't,' he confirmed with a sensual growl, and her body responded with a shiver at remembered pleasure.

'You don't give up, do you?' she charged with an exasperated laugh, genuinely amused despite everything.

Joel leant forward across the table, holding her eyes with his. 'Well, now, that's because you haven't given me any of the signals that would tell me I should.'

Her brows rose, posting a challenge. 'I said no.'

'You didn't mean it, though,' he countered smoothly, and she had no comeback because he was right.

'If I didn't mean it, why did you stop?' she asked curiously, and Joel reached out to brush a finger tenderly over her lips.

'Because, as you said, I'm a gentleman, and you're not quite ready yet.'

The tantalising remark begged a response, and got it. 'Not quite ready for what?'

'For the next step,' he told her simply, and she shook her head in bemusement.

'But *you'll* know when I am, right?'

Joel's smile was chock-full to the brim with male confidence. 'My instinct hasn't failed me yet.'

She was damn sure she didn't like being thought of

as a sure thing. Even now she had a choice. He hadn't 'won' yet. 'There's always a first time. This could be it,' she pointed out coolly.

'Kathryn, sweetheart, there is no *if* any longer, only *when*. If you're honest, you'll admit it. Which is why I'm willing to play the game.'

God, the last thing she needed right now was to be reminded that this was all just a game to him. With a snort of disgust, Kathryn pushed her mug away and rose to her feet. 'You know something, Joel. Just when I think I'm actually beginning to like you, you go and say something so arrogant I could hit you.'

Laughing, he got to his feet, too. 'You already do like me, or you wouldn't get so mad.'

Kathryn sighed helplessly, because of course he was right. Damn it, she more than liked him; she loved him. 'There's probably a latent streak of insanity in my family and it's just manifesting itself,' she declared sardonically.

The message in the warmth of his gaze was unmistakable. 'Call it what you like. Just accept that we'll end up where we both want to be very soon now.'

He was probably right about that, too, but she wasn't about to say so. 'I think this is where I make a dignified retreat. I'm going to dress and get working on retrieving your precious files. At least the computer is always logical, and it doesn't answer back,' she sniped, but with the faintest hint of a smile curling the edges of her mouth. It was impossible to stay angry with him for long.

'How boring,' Joel returned as she headed for the door. She paused with her hand on the knob and glanced back at him.

'How restful,' she countered, and quickly pulled the

door to after her. She couldn't hear Joel laughing, but
she guessed he probably was. Sighing, she headed for
the stairs and went up to her room.

Safe inside, she felt the strength of purpose which
had got her through those last minutes with him evap-
orate, leaving her feeling drained. She made no move
to get dressed but instead curled herself up against the
headboard, sweeping up a pillow to wrap her arms
around as she took time out to ponder the discovery she
had made. Had it really only been mere minutes ago?
The knowledge filled her like an eternity.

She had fallen in love with Joel. It ought not to be a
shock but it was, and she was still reeling from it.
Although she had always known love would strike her
like this, she hadn't expected it to strike her here and
now, with this man. A man who, whilst he loved
women, did not believe in the kind of love which had
just dislodged her world from its foundations. There
was no denying he felt a powerful attraction, one she
felt too, but there was a subtle difference in what they
felt. She had fallen in love with him. Never for a second
did she doubt it. There was something extra where she
was concerned. That indefinable something which put
what she felt beyond the scope of any attraction she had
felt before. That something was the magic ingredient
which told her she had fallen in love.

Unfortunately, love wasn't part of Joel's equation. So
far as he was concerned, what was on offer was a little
harmless affair to pass away the time. Had her heart not
been engaged, she would perhaps have seen it in that
light, too. The strength of their mutual attraction might
have made her revise her notion of what was acceptable.
Now that her heart was ruling her emotions, they were
no longer playing the same game. There was more at

stake than her self-respect. To have a brief affair with a man you were physically attracted to was one thing. To have one with a man you had fallen in love with was quite a different proposition.

Deciding what she was going to do about it had consequences she couldn't ignore. Which was a cruel joke. What *could* she do about it? It wasn't as if she had multiple choices. There were, in fact, only two. To sleep with him, or not to sleep with him. To have something to remember, or nothing. Common sense said it would be less painful in the long run to call it quits now, but to do that would require more strength of will than she knew she possessed. It would be like cutting her heart out. How could she do that, when this was what she had been searching for her whole life? Maybe it hadn't turned out the way she'd expected. He didn't love her and never would, but that didn't change how *she* felt. She loved him, and the blunt fact was that this time would never come again.

From the moment of revelation it had been too late to walk away with her heart intact. It never would be again. She could go, but she would be leaving the greater part of herself behind. Somewhere down the road she would meet someone else and love him as much as she was able, but it would never be like this. It couldn't be, for she would never be heart-whole again. The irony was that meeting Joel had given her something precious, but she would be forever incomplete.

Could she hurt any more or any less if she denied herself this moment?

Put quite simply, Joel Kendrick was the love of her life. Any time with him, no matter how short, had to be worth it. She had to seize the moment and have no regrets.

At the back of her mind a voice insisted that the potential for disaster was great. But it was a small voice, and, as often happens to small voices, it went unheeded.

CHAPTER FIVE

THE snow stopped about midday, and not very long afterwards Kathryn, who was once again ensconced in the study, finally heard the sound of the tractor working down on the road. Her fingers stilled on the keys. It ought to have been music to her ears, but the message it conveyed was that she should be able to leave tomorrow, and it brought the act of parting from Joel too close for comfort. It was ridiculous, really, but after only yesterday wishing for the snow to stop so that she could leave, today she would have been only too happy for it to have gone on snowing indefinitely. The proverb was right when it said you had to be careful what you wished for because you would probably get it.

Sighing, she turned her attention back to the screen. This morning she had checked out Magda's database, just in case the woman had made copies of the files for herself, but she had been innocent of that. Now she was attempting to log into Gray's system. Which was proving to be something of a challenge. The man had state-of-the-art security installed. Of course, no program was fail-safe, but it made getting in as difficult as possible. Most hackers probably wouldn't waste the time, but she had a purpose, so kept plugging on.

'Lunch will be ready in fifteen minutes,' Joel declared, poking his head round the door and making her nearly jump out of her skin.

Pressing a hand to her throat, Kathryn turned and glared at him. 'Don't do that! Creeping up on a person can give them a heart attack!' Not to mention the way he looked. The chunky black sweater he wore along with his denims and boots gave him a rugged, outdoorsy look and was incredibly sexy. Her eyes ate him up, and, seeing it, he grinned.

'I'm glad you like what you see, sweetheart, because I do, too. The picture of you in those leggings that seem to make your legs go on for ever will keep me warm when I'm outside shovelling snow this afternoon.'

She quirked an eyebrow at him. 'A coat, hat and gloves will keep you warmer.'

'Only on the outside, darling. Only on the outside. Now, don't forget. Fifteen minutes. Don't make me come and get you,' he added, and departed with the threat hanging in the air.

He might have gone, but the memory of him lingered, keeping her warm on the inside, just as he had said she would do to him. It was difficult to concentrate after that, but somehow she managed it. Time lost all meaning, and she was progressing well when suddenly the door was thrust open again, and she looked round with a start.

'That's it,' Joel declared sternly. 'Come and eat now,' he ordered.

'But you gave me fifteen minutes!' she protested.

'That was half an hour ago. You need a break, Kathryn.'

'But I'm almost there,' she argued, pointing at the screen. 'Give me a few more minutes,' she begged, hating to leave now, with her goal in sight.

Joel's response was to grab the chair and pull it away from the desk, then bend down and scoop her up in his arms. 'Sorry, but you've run out of time,' he stated firmly, swinging round and striding from the room.

With a gasp of alarm Kathryn put her arms up around his neck. 'Brute! How dare you?' she wailed, but in truth the novelty of being carried in his arms smothered any real sense of annoyance she felt.

A whimsical smile curved her lips. My, but he was strong. He carried her easily, and she was no light-weight. Nobody had ever actually done something like this to her before, and it made her feel kind of soft and molten inside. Without volition her arms tightened their hold fractionally, and she allowed her gaze to study the strong cut of his jaw. He was a man of strength in more ways than one.

'Are you always this masterful?' she asked in a play-ful little voice, and he flickered her a glance as his lips twitched.

'Only with women who can't be trusted to do what's in their own best interests,' he responded as he pushed through the kitchen door. The aroma of hot tomato soup assailed her nostrils and her stomach rumbled.

'So you don't usually do this "Me Tarzan, You Jane" act?' she teased as he set her down on a chair.

He crossed to the cooker, where a saucepan sat with its contents gently bubbling. 'You seem to have brought out a latent protective instinct,' Joel returned wryly, la-dling soup into waiting bowls and bringing them to the table. Placing one before her, he nodded at the spoon. 'Eat, Kathryn.'

'Another order?' she asked, though she did pick up the spoon. Smelling the soup had reminded her how hungry she was.

'A request,' he ameliorated, setting down his own bowl and taking the seat opposite her. But he didn't start eating himself until she had begun. 'Help yourself to bread.' He pushed over a plate with chunky slices of bread piled on it.

'There's enough here to feed a small army,' she remarked ironically, but took a chunk, ripping off a piece which she dunked and then popped into her mouth with a sigh of satisfaction. 'Mmm, delicious. I was ready for this.'

'Then why didn't you come when I told you?' Joel charged, and she shrugged and grinned.

'I forgot.'

'Do you often forget to eat?' he asked curiously, and Kathryn nodded.

'I get caught up in things, and the next thing I know, the day has gone. I look on it as an occupational hazard,' she admitted.

He watched her eat for a while, clearly amused by the way she was tucking in. When she reached for another slice of bread, he laughed. 'My child, you need looking after.'

Startled, she looked up, the spoon hovering at her mouth. 'Are you offering?' she asked, the question slipping out before she could think better of it. Her heart flinched anxiously as she expected a short, sharp response, but to her surprise Joel shrugged.

'Why not? Somebody's got to do it,' he declared evenly, and she set the spoon down in her bowl with a little plop.

Kathryn felt curiously giddy, and didn't quite know what to make of that unexpected reply. It would be so easy to read too much into it, and she couldn't afford to do that. Better to err on the side of caution, she decided, and treat it as a joke.

'Why, Joel Kendrick, that almost sounded like a commitment!' she exclaimed mockingly, whilst deep inside her her heart waited in an agony of anticipation to know just what he meant.

He smiled. 'Only in the short term. Whilst you're here I'm going to make it my number one priority to make sure you eat decently and on time.'

Hope died painfully, and she could only pray it didn't show on her face. 'As I should be leaving tomorrow, weather permitting, that hardly amounts to much.'

'I was hoping to persuade you to stay a little longer,' he returned smoothly, and her heart lurched.

It was something to know that he didn't want her to leave so soon, but it fell way short of what, in her heart of hearts, she was hoping for. 'I can't. I have commitments. And whilst I can reschedule tomorrow's meetings with clients, it wouldn't be very professional of me to cancel them indefinitely just for my own amusement,' she refused, hoping to see disappointment on his face, but his expression was bland.

'Then I'll just have to make the most of the time that you are here.'

It was Kathryn who was disappointed, and she lowered her eyes to her soup, forcing herself to take another spoonful although her appetite had quite vanished. His remark was hardly encouraging to a woman who had, however foolishly, fallen headlong in love with him.

'What are you thinking?' Joel asked after a while, and she glanced up with a wry smile.

'I'm thinking that I must be crazy to even consider getting involved with you,' she replied, telling the truth.

'So you are considering it?' He latched on to that with a speculative gleam in his eye.

She met the look square-on. 'Like I said, I must be crazy,' she said with a wry twist of her lips.

Reaching across the table, he took her hand. 'Sometimes crazy is the only way to be,' he said with soft persuasion, his thumb running caressingly over her skin.

Her eyes searched his for any sign of emotion, but she was fast coming to realise he only let her see what he wanted her to see. 'Have you ever done anything crazy, Joel? I mean personally, not in business. Have you ever knowingly walked out onto a rickety limb and trusted that it wouldn't break?' That was what she felt as if she was doing. It was scary but she would do it anyway, for a faint heart never won anything of value.

A frown creased his brow. 'That sounds like a loaded question. What exactly are you asking me, Kathryn?'

She could have retreated, but she chose not to. 'I guess I'm asking have you ever put yourself in someone else's hands and trusted them not to let you down?'

His frown deepened, and he released her hand, sitting back in his chair. 'If this is about you and me, I can only assure you that I would never hurt you.'

'Not knowingly, I agree. But has it ever occurred to you that you could? For instance, how do you know that I'm not in love with you right now?' she asked daringly, and her heart thudded sickeningly in her chest, then squeezed painfully when he laughed.

'Because I told you it would be a waste of time.'

Kathryn sat back in disbelief. Had he really said that? Of all the answers he could have given, that had to be the most unexpected. 'You think that's all it would take?' she asked incredulously. 'A word of warning from you, and a woman switches her heart off?'

He shrugged. 'It's as good a reason as any. Women tend to fall in and out of love at the drop of a hat anyway.'

This wasn't at all what *this* woman who had fallen in love with him wanted to hear. 'Your cynicism is frightening. I think it's just as well I'm not in love with you,' she lied, out of necessity. If she told him the truth, she was sure he would be kind, but it was possible to kill with kindness. 'I imagine you think one lethal cut is less painful than a thousand small ones when you end a relationship, too.'

'The pain, if there is any, should be over more quickly,' he responded blandly.

Thunderstruck, Kathryn stared at him in total silence. 'You're right, you'll certainly never fall in love if you believe that,' she declared at last.

He shrugged that off, too. 'I told you I wouldn't. I try not to inflict pain, but if I have, then I'm sure it passes the instant a new man comes along,' he told her mockingly, and it rankled.

'You do yourself a disservice. I don't think you'd be that easy to forget,' she retorted tartly, deeply hurt by his attitude. Women were no more fickle than men, and, for both sexes, the heart did not easily forget. 'Honestly, have you never regretted ending a relationship with even one woman?'

'Regrets are a waste of time and energy. I never allow myself to have them,' he answered simply, and a lump settled in her stomach at his ability to cut himself off from all emotion. It made her want to strike back and get some reaction from him.

'Have you heard of hubris? It's the sin of pride. I have this awful feeling that one day you're going to come down to earth with a bump. It will probably be painful, but at least you'll be back with the rest of us mortals.'

Laughing softly, Joel gathered up the dirty dishes. 'If it happens, I'll let you be the first to say I told you so,' he teased, carrying the crocks to the sink, where he quickly rinsed them and stacked them in the dishwasher. 'Right,' he said, turning back to her, 'I'm off outside to get started on the paths now the snow's stopped. You're welcome to join me.'

Kathryn stood up with a shake of her head. 'It's a job which uses more brawn than brain, and that's your department. I'll get back to the computer,' she refused with a sweet smile, and left him there, carrying back to the study a mental picture of him standing by the sink giving that laugh which always chased goosebumps up and down her spine.

Back in the study, Kathryn didn't immediately continue her search, for her thoughts were too full of what had passed between them in the kitchen. He had been cold to the point of being clinical in his determination to keep emotional ties out of his life. She frowned as something nagged away at the back of her mind. Finally it came to her, the contradiction in what he had just said. His opinion of her sex was far from flattering. Women were fickle, falling in and out of love, their emotions so shallow that any hurt they did feel would fade when the next man came along. It was strange reasoning for a man who had implied his faith in women was scant because they only saw him as a money machine.

At that point Kathryn's mind began whirling over past conversations. Joel had said once that no one woman had made him the way he was, yet she was beginning to think otherwise. He liked to give the impression that he couldn't be hurt. Nothing meant anything to him. Yet time and again he'd proved he wasn't a cold man. Inside there was a warm human being who could be kind and thoughtful in so many ways. So why did he give this impression that he wasn't? Because he had once been hurt very badly, and was determined not to be again?

Her eyes widened. That would explain the apparent contradictions. He *had* once trusted someone, and they *had* let him down. He had put up defences, as anyone would, and the wall he had erected to ward off hurt had become thicker and higher over the years, so that now very little dented it.

Which would explain a lot, but didn't exactly help her much. If she was correct, she was in love with a man determined not to love again. She didn't have trumpets to bring his walls crashing down. She only had her love for him, and if that didn't make a chink in his armour, then nothing would. She could not make him love her; she could only hope that he would want to be with her for longer than a few days. Of course, she could always hope for a miracle, but they were a scarce commodity these days. The unhappy truth was, nothing had changed, and his determination was such that in her heart she doubted that it ever would. Love didn't always find a way.

Sighing, she accepted that she had no answer to her own problem. Joel's, on the other hand, she could do something about. Brooding was pointless; better to concentrate on getting into Gray's database. Pushing all other thought to the far reaches of her mind until she could give them the time and care they needed, she forced herself to concentrate on the job at hand. Meeting yet another barrier, she was balked at every turn as she tried to circumvent it. Nothing worked until she had a brainwave. Following it up, the screen suddenly cleared and she was in.

She ran a search for the files and found them surprisingly easily. Gray obviously hadn't expected to be suspected, or that Joel would return the favour by having Kathryn follow Magda's example. All she had to do now was download them onto disks, wipe the files and any backups there were on the hard disk, and her job was done. Restoring them to Joel's computer was a cinch, and when she finally closed the system down, she did so with the satisfaction of a job well done.

Locking the disks in a drawer, she rose and stretched, then went off in search of Joel to tell him the good news. Collecting her coat and gloves from her room, she let herself out of the house and followed the sound of shovelling around the side of the building. Joel hadn't spotted her yet, and she paused, watching him work. He had slipped on a red plaid body warmer over his sweater, and the effect was exceedingly easy on the eyes. He wasn't the most handsome man she had ever met, but she suspected he would be the only one who could make her heart go bump just by the way he used a shovel! If that wasn't a sign she had it bad, then she didn't know what was.

She must have made some sound or movement, for he glanced up suddenly and caught her in the act. Straightening, he used the shovel as a prop and smiled quizzically.

'You look like the cat who ate the cream,' he remarked cheerfully. 'Does this mean you have good news?'

'Um-hm. Your files are back where they belong, and I've locked disk copies in your desk drawer. I don't suppose anything like this will happen again, but to be on the safe side I think you ought to have some security installed,' Kathryn suggested, and he nodded.

'Better late than never. Can you arrange it?'

'There are several programs on the market, or I could

devise one for you. Of course I'd have to send it on to you, with instructions for setting it up.'

Joel leant both arms on the shovel and crossed one foot over the other. 'Still intending to leave tomorrow?'

She would stay for ever if he asked, but he wouldn't. Not now, and probably never. 'I've done what I came to do,' she answered simply.

'What about the unfinished business between us?' he reminded her softly, and the words went right to her heart.

Kathryn lifted an eyebrow and smiled faintly. 'Maybe it would be better remaining that way—unfinished,' she suggested, and was mildly amused to see him straighten up.

Joel's reply was uncompromising. 'Not for me it wouldn't.'

His vehemence was good for her soul, but she didn't allow it to show. Folding her arms, she pretended to give the subject more thought. 'I don't know, a woman ought to keep her mystery. Perhaps I should leave you wondering about what you might be missing,' she proposed provocatively, and he growled low in his throat, rather like a peevish big cat. She laughed outright. 'Now, now. Little boys who throw tantrums are certain not to get their own way.'

Something dangerous flickered in his eyes as he tossed the shovel aside. 'But I'm not a little boy, as you are going to find out,' he promised, advancing on her with clear intent in his wicked grin.

Kathryn's heart leapt, and with a squeal she turned and ran, laughing helplessly at her inelegant efforts to escape over snow-covered ground. Seeing a path to her left, she headed for it.

'No, Kathryn!' Joel called out sharply, but she ig-

nored him and in the next instant felt her legs fly out
from under her. There was barely time for her to cry
out in alarm before she hit the ground with enough force
to knock the air out of her. Seconds later, Joel dropped
to his knees at her side, his expression shocked and
grim. 'Are you OK, sweetheart? Did you hit your head
at all? Talk to me, Kathryn!' he ordered when she re-
mained silent, his hands beginning to run over her,
searching for possible injury.

'What happened?' Kathryn croaked out, now that she
had her breath back, and Joel sat back on his heels,
puffing out a relieved breath.

'Black ice is what happened. It's always under the
snow on this path because it holds water. Are you sure
you're OK?' he asked in concern, frowning as he helped
her sit up.

Kathryn winced. 'Apart from having a bruise which
will make it uncomfortable for me to sit down for a
week, I'm fine,' she reassured him wryly, probing
tender spots and wincing occasionally.

'I could always…' Joel began, but her head shot
round, her eyes flashing a warning as she saw the gleam
in his.

'No, you couldn't,' she declared firmly. 'No part of
my anatomy needs kissing better, thank you very
much.'

He didn't deny that that was what he'd been going
to say. 'There's no need to snap my head off. I didn't
make you fall over.'

Kathryn shot him an old-fashioned look. 'No, but you
would have done if it had been to your advantage.'

Joel grinned. 'Whilst I might want you on your back,
sweetheart, there's a more subtle way of going
about it.'

There was something in the way he said 'sweetheart' that chased goosebumps up and down her spine. The man had everything. 'I've no doubt you know every art of seduction ever invented, and then some,' she returned mockingly, and he tutted.

'The way you say that makes me out to be some kind of modern-day Casanova,' he protested in hurt tones, and she gave him a look which told him he wasn't fooling her one bit.

'No, but you'd run him a close second,' she riposted, laughing softly as she probed another sore spot. Glancing up, she found him watching her with the strangest look in his eyes. 'What?' she asked in confusion, and Joel looked at her with a faint frown.

They were facing each other by now, and he reached out and cupped her cheek with infinite tenderness. 'I was just thinking how much I love your laugh,' he confided, and a frisson of excitement skittered along her nerves.

Suddenly she didn't feel like laughing. 'You pick your moment to tell me. We're sitting in a snowdrift, risking hypothermia,' she said in a breathless little voice.

His hand snaked round behind her neck and inexorably began to draw her closer. 'Are you cold?'

'Only on the outside,' Kathryn admitted huskily, and a smile curved the edges of his mouth upwards.

'Good, because I'm just going to have to kiss you,' Joel growled when they were no more than a breath apart.

Her hands fastened onto his body warmer as she leant towards him. 'What took you so long?' she demanded in little more than a whisper, and then his mouth took hers and the world spun away.

It was a deep, soul-searching kiss that seemed to be seeking an answer from her, though she doubted if he knew the question. She didn't either, so all she could do was respond to it with every ounce of the love she felt for him. It appeared to be what he wanted, for with a low moan he folded his arms around her and drew her across his knees, igniting the fire of their desire with the ever mounting passion of his kisses. Her eyes shut, caught up in the maelstrom, Kathryn responded blindly, and it was only when Joel lifted his head with a muffled curse that the world returned and she realised somewhere close by a bell was ringing insistently.

'It's the telephone again,' he explained, taking a steadying breath. 'I fitted up a speaker so I can hear it when I'm outside.' The ringing stopped, but he was still listening as he set her aside. A few seconds later, it rang again.

Shivering now that the heat of his body had been withdrawn, Kathryn scrambled to her feet. 'I had no idea your work was so important,' she remarked as he followed her up and headed for the house. She tagged along behind, more than a little peeved that he could so easily break off making love to her for the sake of his business.

'This is not about work.' He corrected her assumption without slowing his stride. 'That particular ring pattern is a signal I arranged because sometimes I ignore calls that might be work-related. I'm part of the local search and rescue team. Somebody could be in trouble, and if they are, in these conditions, time is everything.'

Kathryn immediately felt like a prize worm for being irritated, and at the same time felt her heart swell with pride that he should be part of such a worthwhile group. She admitted to being surprised, but, then again, knew

she shouldn't be. She was beginning to learn that he
was a man who gave of himself generously, it was only
where his heart was concerned that he posted 'Keep
Out' signs.

Entering the kitchen, Joel snatched the receiver off
the wall phone. 'This is Joel. What's up?' He asked the
question briskly, then listened intently with lowered
head to whoever was on the other end of the line. 'I'll
be there in twenty minutes,' he said finally, and hung
up.

'Is it bad?' Kathryn asked when he turned and she
could see the serious expression on his face.

'Three walkers were out on one of the crags. Two
fell and could have God knows what sort of injuries.
The third managed to reach a farm and sent out the
alarm. Damn it, it doesn't seem to matter how many
weather warnings are put out, some idiots always manage to ignore them and we have to go and pick up the
pieces.'

Kathryn felt her heart clench in sudden anxiety as she
realised just what rescuing the injured walkers would
mean. 'Won't it be dangerous for you, too?' she asked
unevenly, and he nodded, confirming her worst fears.

'Of course it will. No matter how well we know these
hills, the weather is the enemy. However, we're com-
mitted to rescuing them. No way could we leave them
there, unless the weather turns so bad we can't see our
hands in front of our faces.'

'But…' She began to protest, only he stopped her by
placing his hands on her shoulders.

'I'm sorry, Kathryn, but I don't have time to talk
now. It will be getting dark soon, and we'll need all the
light we can get.' With that he walked round her and

out of the room. As she stood there, biting her lip, she heard him taking the stairs two at a time.

Her instinct was to tell him not to go, for she had this awful mental picture of him tumbling down a sheer cliff and breaking his neck. It made her blood run cold. Yet she knew, if she said it, it would change nothing. Joel would still go. So she held the words back, though her stomach was churning anxiously. When she heard Joel come back down the stairs, she went out to meet him. He was dressed in heavy-duty climbing gear and carried a backpack. Seeing her strained face, he smiled.

'Don't worry, I'll be fine. With any luck they won't be too hard to find, or too badly injured.'

'Be careful,' she advised, her smile a wobbly thing at best, and he bent and pressed a swift, hard kiss on her lips.

'I always am. I'll be back before you miss me,' he added, then turned on his heel and left her.

Kathryn pressed a hand to her lips, for they had an alarming tendency to tremble. She missed him already. She had no doubt he had done this many times before, but she hadn't been in love with him then. He was risking his life to save that of somebody who shouldn't have been out there in the first place, and that made her both angry and frightened. She had absolutely no control over the situation. All she could do was sit and wait, and pray that he came back in one piece.

It wasn't easy. She went upstairs and changed into dry clothes, then spent the next hour wandering aimlessly from room to room, constantly looking out of the window, hoping to see his four-by-four returning, though her brain knew it was far too soon for that. Finally she decided to be positive, and went back to the kitchen, searching the freezer for something to cook for

dinner. He would be back by then, she told herself
firmly, as she defrosted some meat and prepared vegetables for a casserole. Something hot and tasty to chase
away the chills of the hillside.

When dusk fell, she went around lighting lamps and
laying the table. The oven was sending out aromas that
ought to have set her mouth watering, but as the minutes
and then hours passed her confidence faltered. Where
was he? What was happening? Turning off the oven,
she paced back to the lounge and stood at the window,
looking out, willing the flash of headlights to beam out
through the darkness. But they didn't. Eventually she
left her post and curled herself up on the couch, cud-
dling a cushion to her chest and watching the pictures
come and go in the fire. When it died down, she built
it up again, determined that Joel should return to a warm
house.

Midnight came and went, and though she fought it
her eyes grew heavy out of the sheer exhaustion of
worry. Unable to fight it any longer, she stretched out
on the couch, still clutching the cushion, and within no
time at all sleep claimed her.

CHAPTER SIX

'KATHRYN?'

The soft sound of her name being gently repeated drew Kathryn from the depths of sleep. Rolling over, she stared blankly at the man who sat on the edge of the couch, one hand resting on the back cushion as he bent over her.

'Joel?' she murmured groggily, rubbing at her eyes. 'What time is it?'

He brushed a stray lock of hair away from her eyes, his gaze running over the lines of her face softened by sleep. 'A little before three. Why aren't you in bed?'

Memory returned with a rush. The emergency call. Her hours of anxious waiting. 'I wanted to wait up for you. How did it go?' Lord, she was so relieved to see him alive and well. Her eyes ate him up, noting the faint signs of weariness about his eyes. She wanted to throw her arms around him and hold him close, but was afraid of how much that would give away. All she could do was lie there and pretend she hadn't been worried to death.

'It went well. Lucky, our dog, found them without too much trouble, thank God.'

If Lucky were here, she would give her the hug she couldn't give Joel. 'And the walkers?'

'One has a broken leg, the other cracked ribs, but apart from the effects of exposure they're OK. They should consider themselves damned lucky.'

'I'm sure they do. Did you read them the Riot Act?'

Joel dragged a weary hand through his hair, 'Pat, our team leader, did that. Not that it will do much good. Some people never learn. We'll probably be out rescuing the same group next year. I don't know why I do it. It's a mug's game.'

This time Kathryn went with her instincts and sat up, slipping her arms around him in an all too brief hug. 'You do it because you'd never forgive yourself if they could have been saved and you'd done nothing.'

He eased her away, looking at her quizzically. 'Is that so?' he queried, running an exploring hand up and down her spine, setting her nerve-endings tingling.

She nodded. 'You're a good man, Joel Kendrick. You'll never get me to believe otherwise.'

'How can you be so sure? You barely know me,' he argued, and she sighed, using her fingers to comb back hair that fell forward over his forehead.

She couldn't tell him it was because her heart knew him. It wasn't what he wanted to hear. All she could do was shrug carelessly. 'I just know. Call it woman's intuition.' He smiled at that, and her eyes dropped to his lips. Before she could think better of it, she pressed her own lips to his in a swift kiss.

Their eyes locked, and all at once the temperature in the room rose by several degrees.

'What was that for?' Joel asked huskily, and she licked her lips, aware that by her action she had instigated a course of events that had only one ending.

'I just felt like it,' she returned, equally huskily.

'Hmm. Is there anything else you feel like doing?' The question was little more than a tantalising growl.

Her heart kicked. 'We-ell, I could think of several things, but you must be exhausted,' she responded, more than a little breathlessly.

His soft laugh shivered over her flesh. 'Sweetheart, right now I don't feel the least bit exhausted,' he confided, his roving hands finding the hem of her sweater and slipping underneath, searing her with the heat of his touch.

Kathryn closed her eyes and moaned softly as her own hands forayed over the breadth of his back and shoulders, delighting in their latent power. 'Aren't you hungry? I made dinner. It won't take a minute to heat up.'

His mouth found the line of her jaw and traced a path of kisses up to her ear. 'Kathryn, Kathryn. What I'm hungry for is already hot,' he sighed, nipping at her earlobe, making her gasp and shiver.

She rubbed her cheek against his. He needed a shave, but she didn't mind. The slight growth of beard only added to his maleness. A faint smile curved her lips as they brushed his ear. 'It will keep—unless you can't wait,' she teased, and he groaned, abandoning his exploration of her back to cup her face in his hands, looking at her with eyes that blazed with barely suppressed passion.

'I've waited long enough as it is. I'm a starving man with a hunger only you can satisfy.'

The confession was music to her ears. 'Then eat,' she invited huskily. 'Everything I have is yours.'

It was all the invitation Joel needed, and he brought his mouth down on hers, kissing her with an almost desperate passion, taking her lips, parting them, seeking out the honeyed depths of her mouth with his tongue. And Kathryn welcomed him wholeheartedly. She wanted this—needed it. Whatever he might feel for her, she loved him, and the only way she could ever show it was in the giving of her body. Tonight they would make love, and it would be precisely that for her.

Joel broke off the kiss long enough to throw some cushions onto the floor before the low burning fire, then he laid her down on the rug and joined her there, taking her in his arms once more. Like a forest fire in a tinder-dry wood, passion needed only the faintest spark to ignite, and within seconds it was blazing. Feverish kisses were soon not enough, and clothes were a barrier that drove Kathryn wild with impatience. She wanted to feel him, touch him, know him in every way there was, and what her hands could find beneath his sweater was not enough. With a grunt of annoyance, she tugged at the sweater, hauling it up, only to meet the barrier of his arms. But they were two minds with a single thought, and Joel moved, sitting up to pull the sweater over his head and throw it across the room.

Meanwhile Kathryn was removing her own sweater, and he took it from her, tossing it to join his own. She would have reached for the front clasp of her bra, but Joel stopped her. Swiftly straddling her hips, he pushed her hands to the floor beside her head before trailing his fingers down the tender inner flesh of her arms and across her chest, finally hovering at the shadowy cleavage between her achingly sensitive breasts. Instinctively her body arched, inviting him to release the clasp and touch her as she longed for him to do. Her lashes fluttered as at last he undid the fastening and peeled the lacy scrap aside. He touched her then, but it was gentle, almost worshipful, and she shifted beneath him, needing more. After what seemed an age, yet was mere seconds, his hands cupped her tumescent flesh, his thumbs finding her turgid nipples and caressing them into aching points.

A whimper of pleasure broke from her as she watched Joel lower his head and take first one nipple and then the other into his hot mouth and lave them with his tongue. Unable to lie there unmoving, Kathryn lifted her hands to the thick dark mass of his hair and clung on as delicious frissons of pleasure chased paths through her body, starting up a throbbing ache deep within her. Then he moved, his lips and hands tracing scorching paths down her body, meeting the barrier of her leggings only momentarily as he tugged them down, and then they were gone, along with the rest of her clothes.

'Beautiful,' he murmured, as he retraced the trail up her legs to the juncture of her thighs, parting them to seek out the hot, moist centre of her, tightening the coils of passion from which there could only be one outcome.

'No. Wait,' Kathryn protested faintly, wanting this to be a shared pleasure. But Joel had other ideas.

'This time is for you,' he insisted throatily, and continued working his magic on her until one last stroke sent her tumbling over the edge.

Heart racing, she lay with eyes closed as the shattered fragments of her senses reformed. Only when Joel came up beside her, one hand gently brushing damp hair from her face, did she open her eyes and look at him reproachfully.

'That wasn't fair,' she sighed, her desire momentarily appeased.

He smiled, his fingers tracing the ridge of her collarbone and its almost transparently silky skin. 'All is fair in love and war,' he argued, and that brought a spark to her eyes.

'Then it's my turn,' she declared, rising up so that he was forced to fall back, and in an instant Kathryn was straddling his body. Grinning dangerously, she met his gleaming blue gaze. 'Scared? You should be, because

I'm going to make you pay,' she promised as her hands ran forays over the taut planes of his powerful chest.

Joel's teeth flashed. 'Do your worst. I can take it,' he retorted, then his breath hissed in through his teeth as she found his flat male nipples and flicked them with her nails.

Smiling with satisfaction now that she had his attention, Kathryn dropped her gaze to his chest. It felt wonderful to touch him with such freedom, and she gloried in the way he responded to her, keeping nothing back. It was immensely arousing, and she felt her desire stir to life again as she set about tantalising him as he had her. Dipping her head she let her lips find his nipples, and her teeth nipped him, bringing a gasp of pleasure from deep in his throat, then her tongue traced lazy circles before flicking back and forth across the sensitised nubs.

Slowly, slowly she traced a moist pathway down over his flat stomach, feeling the tension grow inside him as she approached the waistband of his jeans. She rose then, her bottom lip caught between pearly teeth as she dealt with the clasp and zip, releasing the aroused male flesh that thrust against his shorts. It was no accident that her hand brushed him as she tugged his pants and jeans down together, and his body jerked up from the floor, a bitten-off curse remaining strangled in his throat. Then she tossed the clothes aside and he lay before her in all his naked male glory. There was no doubting his wanting of her, and she felt her own body start to throb with awakened desire.

It was no longer easy to keep her movements slow and tantalising. Her hands trembled faintly as she ran them over his thighs, getting closer but never quite reaching the place she instinctively knew he wanted her to. Finally she relented, and, as he had done to her, she caressed him, driving him inexorably towards the edge. Joel moaned aloud, and reached for her.

'No more!' he gritted out through clenched teeth as her head came up, and she looked at him, meeting the fiery blaze in his eyes. Knowing he could take no more, Joel clasped her hips, holding her to him as he sought to keep some measure of control.

'Joel.' His name was an ache of longing on her lips, and with it his immense control finally broke. He pulled her down, rolling over so that she was beneath him at last, and he claimed her with one powerful thrust. The presence of him inside her made her feel complete for the first time in her life, and Kathryn clung on, matching his thrusts, seeking an ending that suddenly overwhelmed her, sending her plummeting out into the vortex on a wave of incredible pleasure. Seconds later Joel joined her, climaxing with a groan that seemed to be drawn from the very depths of his being.

Clinging together, they rode out the stormy seas of passion until at last they washed up on the shore, replete and exhausted.

It was a long time later that Joel stirred and became aware that he still lay on top of her. Shifting to one side, yet seemingly unwilling to release her, he hauled her in to his side, settling her head on his shoulder. Then he closed his eyes, and within seconds was asleep. Poised on the edge of sleep herself, Kathryn sighed and laid her hand over his heart.

'I love you,' she whispered, needing to say it and safe in the knowledge that he could not hear her. Then, closing her eyes, she followed him into sleep.

*   *   *

She was jerked awake abruptly, hours later, and lay still with heart thumping as she tried to work out what was happening. Her back was warm, and she realised that some time during the night they had shifted; now Joel lay sleeping with his body cupped around hers, spoon-fashion. She became aware of other things. The room was warm, although the fire had gone out, which meant the central heating had kicked in. Just as well, as they were both lying as naked as the day they were born.

Her lips quirked, but an alien sound quickly wiped it away. It was the sound of a door closing, followed by the unmistakable sound of a car driving away. In a flash she realised that it could only be Agnes returning, and she was sure that in a few minutes or less she would be walking into the sitting-room, where the sight which would reach her eyes would be intensely embarrassing for all concerned.

Looking around desperately for something to cover them with, she caught sight of a throw folded over the arm of a chair. Footsteps crossed the hall as she reached for it and hastily shook it out over them. It didn't cover everything, but enough for modesty, which was just as well—for in the next instant the door was being opened and Agnes came in.

Their eyes met, one pair in surprise, the other in dismay. Yet though her cheeks were burning hot enough to start a fire, she didn't want Joel to wake up. He had had a busy night, what with one thing and another. So she held her finger to her lips to prevent Agnes from saying anything, and indicated that she would join her outside in a moment. At first she thought the other woman would not comply, but in the end she turned and quietly left the room again.

Kathryn eased herself away from Joel, freezing when he murmured something in his sleep, but he merely turned over and she scrambled to her feet, pausing only to drape the throw over him so that he didn't get cold. Dressing took some time, as her clothes were scattered about the room, but less than ten minutes after Agnes had arrived Kathryn left the room and went in search of her. She found her in the kitchen making tea.

Agnes paused long enough to give Kathryn a speaking look. 'I hope you know what you're doing,' she said forthrightly, though there was neither reproof nor dismay in her tone.

Kathryn combed her dishevelled hair with her fingers and folded her arms defensively. 'I think I do,' she responded, feeling uncomfortable at having been found in a compromising position.

Setting the pot of tea on the table, Agnes quickly produced cups and saucers, milk and sugar, then indicated Kathryn should take a seat. She joined her, but said nothing until two steaming cups had been poured out, then she sighed and looked Kathryn squarely in the eye.

'I love Master Joel, but I'm not blind. He plays with women. I've seen them come and go. Some, quite frankly, I was glad to see the back of, and others I thought might make him a good wife. A few of them even loved him, but the majority didn't. They used him, and one by one they changed him from the loving boy I remember. One in particular…' She broke off, biting her lip uncertainly, and Kathryn held her breath, because from the demeanour of the other woman it was obvious there was something she should know.

'What about her?' she probed carefully, and Agnes looked at her sombrely.

'I'm telling you this because I like you, and I can see

you're a good girl. He won't let himself fall in love
with you because of that woman. I could see she was a
flighty piece, but he was crazy about her. They were to
be married until he discovered her with another man.
One she was in love with but who didn't have Joel's
money. The idea was that she would eventually get a
divorce, and the pair of them would live on her settle-
ment. As if that wasn't bad enough, when Joel broke it
off, she got her revenge by telling him she had aborted
his child. Was quite blatant about it,' Agnes revealed
with a shudder of distaste.

Kathryn gasped, horrified. She had been right to suspect there was a woman behind Joel's attitude, but she
could never have suspected this. 'Oh, dear God, how
could she?' That was something she could never do.

'Easily, because she was a cold, evil woman. It sent
him crazy for a while, and we all despaired of him.
Then he sobered up, and when he did there was a wall
around his heart inches thick, and it's getting thicker
year by year. Love doesn't exist for him. He won't let
anyone get close, and that will destroy the woman who
loves him. He will be kind, and generous, but he will
keep his heart locked away. I've seen it happen before,
and I don't want to see it happen to you,' Agnes said
gently, as if she knew Kathryn's secret.

'What makes you think it will?' she charged, trying
to keep her voice steady, but it wavered tellingly.

Agnes sipped at her tea carefully, then looked at her
over the top of the cup. 'Because you're here and he
isn't. Your thoughts are for him, not yourself.'

Kathryn felt heat rise in her cheeks again, and knew
how revealing that was. 'He had to go out onto the hills
yesterday, for a rescue, and didn't get in until this morning. I thought he needed the sleep.' She explained away

her actions, but Agnes was no fool, as was becoming clear.

'Maybe, but most of the others would have woken him and sent him out to deal with me and cover their blushes.'

Kathryn didn't want to be reminded of the others, and refused to think of those who would come after her. She was with him now. This was her time. 'I'm not like the others.'

Agnes reached out and patted her hand kindly. 'No, you're not. I only wish I could believe it would make a difference.' She sighed and shook her head sadly. 'I'm afraid Master Joel won't change.'

Kathryn stirred her tea for a second in silence, then sighed. 'You're right, I do love him,' she said honestly. 'But he'll never hear that from me. He must never know, and you must promise not to tell him either. You see, I don't expect him to love me. He's made that quite clear. So as far as he's concerned, this is just another affair. I know it's going to hurt when it's over, but it would hurt a lot more if he was to pity me. I believe I can take anything but that,' she added with a wince, and Agnes's expression changed to one of compassion.

'Don't get yourself into a fret. I'm no tattletale. Your secret is safe with me,' she promised. 'I wish there was something I could do, but it's gone too deep with him. I'll pray for you, though. Pray that he comes to his senses and sees what's staring him in the face. You'd be good for him. I can only hope he will come to see that, too.'

Silence fell then, for there was nothing more to say. By mutual consent they chatted about other things for a while, then Kathryn excused herself to go upstairs to shower and change—and pack for the journey home.

She looked in on Joel on the way, but he was still sleeping soundly, and she hadn't the heart to wake him, though she was sorely tempted to. Waking in his arms and making slow passionate love together would have been something to take away with her, but his need for sleep was greater, so she carefully closed the door again and continued on her way.

As she showered she did her best to remain positive, but she had no idea where they went from here. Last night had been magical, but how could it be repeated when they lived at opposite ends of the country? How could they continue an affair at a distance? She didn't believe it could be done, and steeled herself to the possibility that last night would quite likely be all there would ever be.

Painful fingers tightened around her heart. It was not enough. It was nowhere near enough. Yet, in all honesty, even a lifetime would fall short. Only an eternity would do, and that was out of the question because of an unknown woman who had all but destroyed him. But for her they might have had a future. She could only imagine how Joel must have felt, and she despised the woman for what she had done to him. Yet it was no use crying over spilt milk, for she could not change the past. All she could do was put on a brave face. If this was the end, then she would bear it somehow.

She was dressed once more and in the process of packing when a sound at the door caused her to straighten and turn. Joel stood in the doorway, the throw draped about him like a toga. With his hair in disarray and a night's growth of beard on his chin, he looked like an ancient Roman version of the morning after the night before. She couldn't help but smile at him, and her heart turned over at the rather endearing effect of his bare feet poking out of the bottom fringe. Her first instinct was to fling herself into his arms and stay there for ever. She resisted it—just—and made do with storing the memory of him in her heart.

'What are you doing?' he wanted to know as he sauntered casually into the room, a mild frown on his forehead.

'Baking a cake,' she riposted, as it must be obvious from the case and pile of clothes on the bed just what she was doing. Picking up a jumper, she folded it neatly and placed it in the case.

'Going somewhere?' he asked next, as she continued to pack.

Though it was the hardest thing she had ever had to do, she made herself respond lightly. Coming on heavy was absolutely the wrong thing to do. 'I have a train to catch, remember. Agnes says the roads are clear, so I'm going home as planned.'

'Agnes is back?' That clearly surprised him. Obviously he hadn't run into her yet. Kathryn felt sure the woman would have something pointed to say to him when he did.

Her lips twitched. 'Um-hm. You were unconscious at the time. She walked in on us. I just had time to cover us with your toga there. Which, by the way, is very fetching. Anyway, it could have been very embarrassing.' It had been embarrassing enough as it was. She picked up another jumper and was about to fold it when Joel caught her wrist, forcing her attention.

'Why didn't you wake me?' he asked a tad testily, and her brows rose.

'Because you needed the sleep. Although I have to admit it hasn't left you in a sweet mood,' she added, looking pointedly at where he held her.

'That's because I expected to find you beside me when I woke up,' he complained, and her shrug hid the fact that she had wanted to wake with him, too. It just hadn't been meant to be.

'As you can see, I had things to do,' she said matter-of-factly, making him frown even harder.

'Are you always this cool after you've spent the night with a man?' he demanded somewhat frostily himself, and she laughed softly, though it was the last thing she felt like doing. Howling better fitted the bill.

'I'm just being sensible. Besides, I thought you weren't enamoured of the clinging type. I'm sorry if I hurt you by leaving you downstairs, but I thought I was playing by the rules,' she replied dryly, and in a flash he had dropped her arm and stepped back, hitching up the toga, which showed a tendency to slip floorward.

'I wasn't hurt,' Joel denied curtly, and Kathryn shot him an old-fashioned look.

'It sure sounds as if you were,' she said, unable to resist taunting him, since he was behaving unreasonably so far as she could see.

'I was disappointed, not hurt. I wanted to make love to you again,' he corrected, his voice dropping an oc-tave seductively, and she felt heat rise in her cheeks at the memory of what they had shared.

'I would have liked that, too,' she admitted huskily.

At her answer, heat dispelled the frost in his eyes, and he closed the gap between them, taking her by the shoulders. 'Then stay,' he urged huskily. 'Stay one more day and we can spend it in bed together. Last night was incredible, wasn't it?'

She drew in a shaky breath. 'Yes, it was,' she agreed honestly. 'You were right, your lovemaking is even more incredible than your arrogance.' She reminded him of what he had said to her mere days ago, and he smiled a crookedly attractive smile.

'If you want the truth, it surpassed even what I expected, and I want to feel that way again. Stay, Kathryn. Please.'

Lord, how she wanted to, but it wasn't possible, and she shook her head, her throat tight with emotion. 'I can't. I told you that. I have commitments.'

'To hell with your commitments!' Joel barked, then, lowering his head swiftly, he pressed a hard kiss on her lips that sent her blood racing through her veins. It was over far too soon and she was left staring up at him.

'If you do that again, you'll probably change my mind, but please don't. My work is important to me, as are my customers. I *have* to go home,' she argued unevenly, and looking down, he gave a resigned sigh.

'Damn, but you're a stubborn woman. You're going to make me wait, and I hate waiting.'

Her heart kicked, for she knew the wait would be longer than he thought. 'Does that mean you want to see me again?' she somehow managed to ask teasingly, whilst inside her stomach tied itself into a nervous knot.

'After last night, how could you think otherwise? This is not the end, Kathryn, but the beginning.'

'Maybe, but I don't know when I can get back here again,' she felt honour bound to point out, and his laugh came as quite a surprise.

'It's flattering to know you want to come to me, but it won't be necessary. I'm cutting my visit short. There are one or two things I have to do, but I'll be back in town at the end of the week. Have dinner with me Friday night.'

Her shock had to be written across her face. 'But…I thought you lived here?'

Joel shook his head. 'No such luck. I spend as much time as I can here, but my work keeps me in London most of the time,' he explained, and she realised that if she had been thinking clearly she would have worked that out for herself. Drew was based in London, so his boss must be, too.

'I see,' she groaned, feeling a fool.

'So, are you going to give me an answer any time soon, or do I have to wait in suspense?' Joel teased with a soft laugh, and when she blinked at him he gave her a tiny shake. 'Dinner. Friday night. Is it a date?'

About to give the swift *yes* her heart demanded, she bit it back in favour of a more flirtatious response. She couldn't let him see how relieved she was. 'I think Friday is free. I'll have to check my calendar.'

Joel's eyes glittered. 'It had better be. In fact, you can keep all your evenings free from now on. I'm not sharing you with anyone,' he declared, sending a thrill of excitement along her nervous system. They were the very words she wanted to hear.

Though she was more pleased by his reaction than she could ever admit, she knew she had to keep some measure of sanity, and she shook her head. 'I'm afraid you're just going to have to share me. I have dinner with my parents at least once a week.'

'That I will allow,' he conceded graciously, and she laughed and pushed herself away from him with a tiny thump on his chest.

'Generous of you. Now, go away and let me finish packing. My train leaves in a couple of hours and I daren't miss it.' She shooed him off, returning to her case and picking up another item with trembling fingers.

'You'll get there on time. I'll take you myself,' he promised, and she glanced at him over her shoulder.

'You don't have to do that,' she protested, though inside her nerves were fluttering like mad.

'Oh, but I do,' Joel insisted as he headed for the door. 'If I have to let you out of my sight for a week, I'm going to make damn sure you have something to remember me by.'

Kathryn stared after his departing back, wishing she could tell him that she would remember him always. It gladdened her heart to know that he didn't want this to be over between them too soon, but oh, how she wished that it didn't have to be over at all. But it was no use crying for the moon. She had to be grateful for what he could give her, and store the memories away so that they could warm her on those long empty nights that surely lay ahead.

CHAPTER SEVEN

A WEEK could seem endless when you were waiting for the weekend to arrive, but it was even longer when you were in love. An hour had never taken so long to pass, nor a day such an eternity. By the time Friday finally came round, Kathryn was a mass of fluttering nerves. Though it had only been a few days since she had seen Joel, and he had called her on the telephone every evening, she had missed him terribly. Eight o'clock seemed so far away. She didn't know how she was going to get through the day.

As is turned out, she had more distractions than she'd anticipated. Firstly somebody called with a problem that couldn't be handled over the phone, and she had to travel to deal with it. That took all morning, but she was home again in time for a late lunch of coffee and a slice of frozen pizza. Not exactly appetising, but Kathryn wasn't really hungry, and was only eating because she knew she'd better put something in her empty stomach.

She was just sitting down at the pine table set in the bay window which made up the dining area of her kitchen, overlooking her tiny garden when the doorbell rang. Answering its summons, she found Drew on her doorstep, a large florist's box in his hands, which he offered to her as he stepped inside.

'Why are you bringing me flowers?' she asked curiously, closing the door and following him back into the kitchen.

'I'm not. I met the delivery boy on the doorstep and offered to give them to you. Who is sending you flowers? Or do I need to ask?' he drawled, with a look that spoke volumes.

A faint pink wash stained her cheeks revealingly. 'I have been known to receive flowers before,' Kathryn countered, setting the box on the table and removing the lid.

'Not from that location, you haven't,' Drew asserted dryly, having noted the address of the high-class florist.

Kathryn wasn't listening to him; she was busy folding back the layers of tissue paper and revealing the exquisite blooms of a dozen long-stemmed red roses. The card lying on them simply said 'Joel', in a strong flourish, and her heart turned over in her chest. Her hand trembled as she picked up one bloom and inhaled the deliciously creamy scent. Her mind was buzzing crazily. Red roses. All the world and his wife knew what they were meant to mean, but she hastily told herself not to read too much into it. Yet they *were* red roses, and that had to mean he cared for her a little, didn't it?

'They are from Joel, I take it?' Drew sought confirmation, watching her cross the room and reach down from a cupboard a crystal vase which she proceeded to fill with water.

'Yes,' she answered simply, setting the vase on the table and looking at him steadily, daring him to stand in judgement.

Drew grimaced. 'Well, that explains why you've been avoiding me,' he declared with a sigh, and she frowned at him.

'I haven't been avoiding you,' she denied automatically although in retrospect that was precisely what she had been doing. With her emotions in a state of upheaval right now, the last thing she needed was to listen to Drew's well-meaning dissertation on why getting involved with Joel was not a good thing.

Drew looked at her askance. 'Leaving your answering machine on all the time smacks of avoidance to me. You haven't returned one of my calls, and that just isn't like you, Kathy.'

She started arranging the roses in the vase, and paused with a sigh. It wasn't like her, that was true. 'I'm sorry,' she apologised, and her cousin came across and slipped an arm around her shoulder, giving her a quick hug.

'Don't worry about it. I guess I don't need to ask how long this has been going on. Since I introduced you,' he said, with a nod to the flowers. 'How serious is it?'

'That kind of depends on your perspective, doesn't it?'

'I've got a pretty good idea what Joel's is, Kathy. Yours, I'm not so sure about.'

Kathryn toyed with a bloom, tracing the silky texture of the petals with her thumb. 'My perspective is very simple. I'm in love with him.'

Drew swore under his breath. 'Damn, I guessed as much. I could kill him!' he added angrily, and Kathryn laid a soothing hand on his arm.

'Joel had nothing to do with it. Not in the way you mean. He believes that, having told me not to fall for him, I won't. Right now, he thinks I feel the same way he does—that this is nothing more than another affair from which we'll both walk away unscathed at the end.'

'Only you won't,' Drew pointed out succinctly, and she didn't argue with him because she couldn't.

'Listen, Drew. I went into this with my eyes open,

and I have no intention of calling foul because my feelings will be hurt. I'm prepared for that.'

Drew pulled her close and sighed heavily. 'Kathy, I love you dearly, but you're a fool. Nobody is ever prepared for that kind of pain. Unfortunately, you're going to find that out the hard way. Just remember I'll be here for you whenever you need me.'

She rested her head on his shoulder. 'Don't tell the family. I don't want them to find out and start asking awkward questions.'

'OK, but they'll find out eventually. Joel is news wherever he goes, and if you're with him, you will be too,' he warned.

'I'll cross that bridge when I come to it,' she declared, easing herself away from him. 'Well, now that you're here, do you want some lunch? I'm having pizza,' she offered with a twinkle in her eye, for she knew how he loved it.

'Pepperoni?' he asked hopefully, and when she nodded he pulled out a chair and sat down. 'You've twisted my arm. Make mine a large slice,' he commanded, and Kathryn was laughing again as she headed for the freezer.

Though it had brightened her day, Kathryn had pushed Drew's visit to the back of her mind by the time eight o'clock came around that evening. The only man she could think of was Joel, and his imminent arrival. She had spent ages agonising over what to wear, nothing had seemed quite right for such a momentous occasion, but in the end she'd plumped for a simple emerald two-piece, consisting of a skirt and matching top with shoe-string straps made out of some silky material.

Of course, then all she had to do was wait, and those

minutes until the doorbell rang seemed to stretch out interminably. When it did ring, her pulse leapt into a gallop, and she had to tell herself quite sternly to play it cool. So it was an outwardly calm Kathryn who opened the door to him, whilst on the inside she was a jumbled mass of nerves. The deep sense of joy it gave her just to see him there twisted her heart, and told her, had there been any doubt, that her feelings hadn't changed.

Joel looked magnificent in a black dinner suit and white silk shirt. With his hands casually tucked into his trouser pockets, he appeared suave and relaxed, not to mention extremely handsome, and the words of greeting she had planned to say were completely forgotten. All she could do was grip the door like grim death as her knees went weak, and say, 'Hello,' in a gruff little voice.

'Hello, yourself,' he returned, with one of those lazy smiles that turned her heart over. She smiled back, drinking him in, and lost track of the passage of time until he quirked an eyebrow at her and said, 'Much as I admire your front step, I'd much rather be inside with you.'

A comment which had her stepping aside to allow him in as a soft flush invaded her cheeks. Idiot, she berated herself silently. She had to pull herself together or her secret would be out of the bag in a flash. 'Oh! Of course. Come in,' she invited, and he did so with a soft laugh.

'I'm flattered you were lost for words. I don't imagine that happens often,' he teased, and she took her cue from that and hastened to recover lost ground.

'Actually, I was trying to decide whether you look more sexy in that suit or the fetching number you wore the other day,' she returned with a touch of irony, referring to the throw he had draped around himself. Closing the door, she sealed them into her compact hallway, which instantly shrank to half its size, heightening the atmosphere considerably.

'And your decision was?' he prompted.

Kathryn leant back against the door, folded her arms and tipped her head to one side consideringly. 'It was close. I'd hate to have to live on the difference,' she said wryly. 'You're looking extremely handsome tonight. Is that for something special?'

His teeth gleamed as he grinned at her manoeuvre. 'Fishing for compliments, sweetheart?'

She pouted prettily. 'You could at least have said I was special.'

Banked fires glowed in the depths of his eyes. 'Oh, you are that, Kathryn, darling. You are most certainly that. But, since you mention it, and now I come to look at you, you're looking pretty delectable yourself. That colour makes your hair gleam like burnished gold. It takes my breath away.'

'Good,' she declared with unabashed satisfaction, allowing her eyes to rove over him at their leisure in the low lighting. 'It's only fair. You've been doing that to me since I met you!'

'Now there's an admission. What else have I been doing to you?' he asked in that gloriously sexy undertone that skittered along her nerves, setting them at attention.

Her brows rose. 'Now who's fishing?'

He laughed. *'Touché.'*

Finally she lifted her eyes to his and held them, unable to resist adding achingly, 'It's been a long week.'

Joel's smile faded too, and as if her words were a

cue he had been waiting for he reached out for her. 'A hell of a long week,' he agreed with a groan, pulling her effortlessly into his arms and taking her lips in a long, deep, soul-searching kiss that she returned in equal measure and which left them breathless but temporarily satisfied when they finally broke apart. 'God, I needed that,' he said thickly, his breathing awry, resting his forehead against hers, and Kathryn linked her hands around his neck and sighed.

'I don't care if you want to know it or not, but I missed you,' she confessed, and Joel settled his hands on her hips, holding her to him so that she could feel the effect she had on him.

'I missed you, too,' he said, surprising her more than a little. 'I didn't expect to, but somehow you got under my skin last weekend and I found myself thinking of you when I should have been concentrating on my work. My secretary was expecting me to come down with flu or something.'

That he had been acting out of character because of her pleased her so much she just had to laugh. 'Poor darling,' she sympathised, but her heart had swelled just a little. Hope, she discovered, could find sustenance from many different sources.

Blue eyes narrowed dangerously, though they couldn't hide the glitter in his eyes. 'So, it amuses you to have me dangling on the end of your string, does it?'

If only he was, she thought wistfully, but this was all part of the game, and she was determined to keep up her side of it. 'It does give me a deliciously feminine sense of power,' she agreed.

'And what, exactly, do you intend to do with it?' came the softly seductive question, sending shivers down her spine.

Kathryn's smile was seduction itself as she toyed with his lapel. 'Well, now…that's for me to know and you to find out,' she said, glancing up at him through her lashes, and he growled low in his throat.

'Did anyone ever tell you you're a dreadful tease?'

Her smiled broadened into a grin. 'Hmm, often, but they didn't seem to mind.'

The declaration had his eyes narrowing. 'I don't think I like the sound of these other men you've twisted round your little finger,' Joel remarked darkly, at which Kathryn laughed huskily, delighted by this merest hint of jealousy.

'It all depends on who *they* are. It just so happens I'm talking about my brothers, so you really don't have to see them as a threat. I'm yours for as long as you want me,' she added lightly, though it was God's honest truth.

There was just the faintest hint of an odd look in his eye as he ran a finger down the bridge of her nose, as if his reaction had surprised him, too. The next second it was gone and he was smiling faintly. 'The way I feel right now, I'll want you for a long time.'

Knowing how he felt, it was all she could realistically hope for. 'Sounds good to me.'

'Your honesty is refreshing.'

Kathryn shrugged lightly. 'I try always to tell the truth, unless it could hurt somebody. Or when I'm trying to put one over on my brothers.'

A mock wary look entered Joel's eyes. 'Ah, your brothers. How many of them are there, did you say?'

'Four. And they're all big. Built like rugby players.' They had, in fact, all played rugby at university, and her eldest brother Nathaniel still did.

'You're just trying to scare me,' Joel charged, which made her laugh.

'Don't say you haven't been warned,' she said, and his eyes widened.

'Am I likely to meet them?'

Knowing her family, Kathryn grimaced inwardly. She wouldn't like to bet against it. 'Sooner than you think when they hear about you,' she said wryly, and that about said it all.

'Ah!'

'Precisely.'

Joel, contrary to her expectations, or maybe not quite that contrary, laughed out loud. 'It looks like I'm in for an interesting time.'

'I'll remind you you said that when you come back gnashing your teeth,' she returned dryly, though she was secretly pleased that he didn't seem bothered by the prospect. Most of the men she had dated had blanched at the thought.

'I get along with most men.'

She sent him a wry look. 'Ah, but you're not sleeping with their sister. It's a bit of knowledge I'd rather they found out later than sooner.' As soon as her father found out, the fat would be in the fire.

Joel placed a finger under her chin and tipped her head up. 'What do you think is going to happen? That they're going to chase me away? It isn't going to happen. Trust me.'

Her smile was unknowingly wistful. 'I do trust you, Joel. I just happen to know my brothers better than you do.'

'OK, I'll grant you that, but if what you say is true then they're my problem, not yours. Forget the Fearsome Four. Tonight I don't want any distractions.

I'm taking you to dinner, as planned, and later we'll go somewhere quiet where I promise you your brothers will be the last thing on your mind.'

He proved to be as good as his word. They dined at a small Italian restaurant, where Joel appeared to know the owners very well. Immediately they arrived the family flocked around their table, issuing greetings in their native tongue, before returning to their various jobs.

'You're very popular. Does that mean you bring all your women here? It would certainly give them a lot of patronage,' Kathryn observed ironically, once they had placed their order, taunted by a stab of jealousy.

Joel tutted reprovingly. 'You can sheathe your claws, sweetheart. This is my private retreat from the glare of the photographers' flashlights. Lorenzo is the son of an old family friend. I loaned him the money to set up his first restaurant. A loan he paid back in good order because he is a proud man.'

Kathryn could have kicked herself for allowing that tinge of jealousy to show through. It wouldn't be so bad if she didn't feel so vulnerable. 'I'm sorry, that was uncalled-for. No wonder you were virtually mobbed,' she apologised gracefully, and his smile was wry.

'Actually, sweetheart, I was mobbed because I've never brought a woman here before, except my mother, and the family wanted to get a good look at you. I should have expected it would cause a stir, but I wanted to take you somewhere where I could have you to myself. Lorenzo will make sure we're not disturbed.'

Kathryn tried not to read anything into that, but it was hard not to. Bringing her to a place he usually reserved for his own privacy was completely unexpected. At the very least it suggested she was different from all the others. Not that she expected it to bring a radical change of heart on his part. She had to be sensible and keep her feet well and truly on the ground or she would only be deepening the heartache that must come at the end of their affair. If she expected nothing, then everything he gave her was a bonus. Like being here tonight.

'Surely there were other restaurants you could have chosen?' she felt compelled to point out, hanging on the answer.

She wasn't disappointed. 'Undoubtedly. But I wanted to bring you here. I thought you would appreciate it the way I do.'

'Oh, I do. It's wonderful. I had no idea it was here. I'm glad the crowd haven't found it yet.' So many places she had gone to had been spoilt by their own popularity.

''Renzo offers two things I find invaluable. Good food in a friendly atmosphere. No smart talk or mobile phones.'

'Don't you use one?' she asked, for most businessmen found them a necessary tool of the trade.

'I do. But when I take a woman out I leave the mobile phone at home, so she can have my undivided attention,' Joel informed her in his lazy drawl, his eyes a sapphire caress.

And his undivided attention was what she got for the rest of the evening. They could have been the only two people in the room, and the food, whilst delicious, couldn't distract them from each other for long. It was late when they finally left. Kathryn had no idea where the time had gone. She settled into his car with a sigh of satisfaction and allowed her thoughts to drift as he set the car in motion. Happiness was a warm bubble inside her, and she felt that way simply by being with him. When the car stopped, she looked around her in surprise.

'Where are we?' she asked curiously. They were parked in a quiet tree-lined street of townhouses.

'My place,' Joel replied, releasing their seat belts. 'I thought we could have a nightcap here before I take you home.'

She looked into his eyes, and even in the darkness she could see the fire burning way down deep inside. Desire had been an unspoken thing between them all evening. The silent companion had been quietly building up, only recognised in a look or a touch, until now it was just below the surface, ready to explode out of control. Kathryn's stomach tightened, starting up that familiar ache inside her. She wanted him desperately.

At the same time her heart skipped, because he was giving her a choice. If she wanted to slow the pace of their relationship, he would take her home now. It was what she was coming to expect of him, but it wasn't what she wanted, for she had waited too long already.

'A nightcap sounds fine,' she agreed huskily, and very briefly he reached out and ran a finger over her lips. Then he was getting out of the car and coming round to help her out. Her heart was racing as they mounted the steps to the front door. In no time at all they were inside with the world shut out.

Without a word Joel tossed his keys onto a small table, then swept her up into his arms and carried her towards the stairs.

'I thought we were having a drink?' Kathryn challenged as her arms slipped around his neck and her lips found the angle of his jaw.

He didn't pause on his way to his bedroom. 'Kathryn, sweetheart, I'm like a man dying of thirst and you're the only thing that will keep me alive. I've kept my hands off you all night. Don't ask me to wait any longer.'

The passion in his voice turned her heart over, and emotions overflowed. 'I won't. Drink. Take all you need.' The spring of her love was never ending. There was more than enough for two.

Inside the bedroom, Joel lowered her to her feet and left her to switch on a lamp beside the bed. Shrugging out of his jacket, he tossed it and his tie aside before striding back to her. Kathryn went into his arms and sighed with satisfaction as his strong arms closed around her. When he bent and took her lips she met his kiss, returning it, sensing the need that he could barely control. It set her heart racing, and her fingers clutched at him, trying to pull him impossibly closer.

This was not like before. There was no slow loving, no languorous build up, for they had been apart too long and their need was too great. They gasped as each breathless kiss supplanted another, their hands dealing feverishly with clothes, discarding them in a staggered trail to the bed where, naked at last, they toppled onto the covers in a tangled mass of limbs. The feel of him against her, the unmistakable evidence of his powerful need thrusting against her belly, scattered Kathryn's senses. She moved against him with a moan, and one muscular male thigh pushed hers apart, allowing him to slip between them and enter her with one thrust.

Kathryn's body arched upwards in pleasure, and her legs rose, locking about his hips as she drew him deeper into her. Joel tried to slow down, she could feel the tension in his body, but the desire was too great, and with a groan he thrust into her again and again, setting up a rhythm she matched, driving them both towards the satisfaction they sought so desperately. It came with explosive force, causing them both to cry out and cling to each other as the waves of pleasure swept over them, drowning them, tossing them in the maelstrom until finally washing them up on calmer shores, where they lay unmoving as the world righted itself again.

At last Joel raised his head and looked down at her, a frown marring his brow as he brushed sweat-soaked strands of hair from her cheeks. 'Are you OK? Did I hurt you?' he asked, and there was genuine concern in his voice, for he had not been gentle.

Kathryn recognised his worry, but she hadn't wanted his gentleness. Only his wildest passion could have been enough. She smiled, lifting a tender hand to cup his cheek. 'You didn't hurt me. You couldn't,' she reassured him.

'You should have stopped me,' he insisted, the frown getting deeper, and she smoothed it away with her fingers.

'I didn't want you to stop. I wanted you just the way you were.'

Reluctantly reassured, Joel rolled off her onto his back and took her with him, settling her over his heart. 'I don't usually lose control like that,' he declared somewhat uneasily.

Kathryn locked that away in her heart, too. 'I'm glad you did. I liked it.'

'Hmm,' he sighed, and yawned. 'Damn, I can hardly keep my eyes open.'

'Go to sleep,' she urged, feeling her own eyelids growing heavy.

'You won't run off this time?'

She laughed softly. 'No. I'll be here when you wake. I promise.' She wasn't about to leave him. If it was up

to her, she would never leave him, ever. Seconds later
she heard the steady sound of his breathing and knew
that he was asleep. Again, knowing that he could not
possibly hear her, she pressed a soft kiss over his heart.
'I love you,' she murmured, just before sleep claimed
her.

Hours later, Kathryn stirred, her hand automatically
reaching out for the body which should have been there
beside her. When her hand encountered only empty
space her eyes shot open and she came up on her elbows. Blinking in the half-light of early morning, she
discovered Joel sitting in a chair by the window. He
must have been awake some time, for he had put on a
knee-length silk robe.

Surprised, she pushed herself up against the pillows
and realised that at some point he had pulled the bed-
spread over her. 'What are you doing over there?' she
asked sleepily. 'Come back to bed,' she urged, holding
out a hand to him.

'Are you on the pill?' he demanded tersely, causing
her to gasp at his tone. There was nothing lover-like in
it, and automatically she pulled the cover more closely
around her protectively.

'No,' she said honestly, wondering what was wrong
and where the conversation was leading. It wasn't at all
what she had expected after the loving they had shared.

'Hell!' he swore abruptly, rising to his feet and pacing across the floor, dragging a hand through his hair,
a clear sign of just how distracted he was.

Kathryn swallowed nervously, picking up on his unease. 'Joel, what's wrong?'

He swung round, and even in the dim light she could
see how grim his expression was. 'I didn't use any pro-

tection last night. Or before. I wanted you too damned much to think of it,' he told her tightly, and now she did think she began to see where this was heading. She hadn't thought of it either—because she'd been blinded by love. But obviously the last thing he needed was for her to have that sort of hold over him, if worse came to worst.

'I see. Well, I doubt very much if anything will happen,' she returned levelly, keeping her composure with an effort. It hurt to think how coolly he could look at their relationship. She had only seen passion. Consequences had been far from her mind. Not so him, apparently.

Joel thrust his hands into his pockets and paced back to her. 'It could. Even now you could be pregnant,' he countered tautly, a nerve ticking away in his jaw.

'Of course I could be—but it's very early in my cycle still, so the risk is small,' she pointed out, and could have sworn she heard him grind his teeth.

'But if you *were*, what would you do?'

Put on the spot, all she could do was shrug helplessly. 'What every other woman would do, I suppose,' she answered, and was astounded to see his face shut down.

'You'd get rid of it, then,' he pronounced coldly, and her face registered her shock because that wasn't what she had meant at all.

'No!' she denied quickly, sitting up to emphasise the point. 'Of course I wouldn't do that!' Emotion tightened her throat. 'How could you think I could do that? God, I couldn't do that to my own child! What sort of woman do you think I am?' she added angrily, coming to her knees and only just remembering to take the bedcover with her. Not for modesty, but because she was too angry to sit there naked.

Her protest had obviously surprised him, and he stared at her through narrowed eyes. 'You wouldn't be the first,' he said tightly, and it was only then that she remembered what Agnes had told her, about his fiancée. The anger died out of her in a rush, and she swallowed hard.

'No, I wouldn't be the first, but I'm not like that. If I were pregnant, I'd keep my baby. I think most women would, given the choice,' she told him with soft insistence, and after staring at her for a moment he turned and walked back to the window, pulling aside the curtain to look out. Even from behind she could see the tension in him, the battle that was going on inside him. Tell me, she urged silently. Let me in. Let me in this much, please.

Whether he heard her or not, Joel dropped the curtain and turned to face her. His expression was so bleak it brought tears to block her throat, and she bit her lip hard.

'You probably think I'm making too much of it, but I have good reason.' He stopped there and took a deep breath, and she knew how hard it was for him to say this. To reveal so much of himself. 'I was engaged once, to a woman who I loved and who I thought loved me. In truth she only wanted my money. When she found out she was expecting my child, she got rid of it,' he told her in a toneless voice, and her heart wept, for beneath it all she could sense his pain, even if he wasn't aware of it. It had hurt then and it still did, which was why he was so troubled now.

'I'm so sorry,' Kathryn said gently, and he looked at her intently.

'I'm not going to allow that to happen again, Kathryn.'

She nodded and licked her lips, wondering if he was aware of all he had said. That he had loved once. She doubted it. Nor would she tell him. She would simply hold on to the thought of it, for what had once happened could happen again. 'That's understandable.'

Sighing, he returned to her, this time sitting down on the edge of the bed. 'I'm usually very careful about using protection, but you have the knack of driving every sane and sensible thought out of my mind. Now you could be pregnant, and, if you are, I want you to promise me that you won't get rid of it.'

Frowning to keep back emotional tears, Kathryn cupped her hand to his cheek and looked him squarely in the eye. 'I've already told you I would never do that, but, if it helps, I give you my word.'

Joel closed his eyes for a moment, and she could only imagine what sort of devil he must have been fighting with. 'You'd tell me if you were pregnant? We may be in the twenty-first century, but I believe a child should be brought up knowing both its parents.'

'I believe that, too,' Kathryn agreed, and, because she couldn't bear to sit there feeling his pain and doing nothing, she cast her arms around his neck and held him close. 'If it happens, I promise to tell you. I would never deny you your child,' she whispered, voice thick with suppressed emotion. Loving him, she could never think of doing that to him. Especially knowing what had happened before. When his arms lifted and encircled her, she closed her eyes tightly, emotions threatening to choke her.

'Thank you,' he said gruffly, and her soft laugh held the faint echo of a sob. 'I'm sorry if I hurt you, but I could only see history repeating itself. I should have known better. I know you're not like her. You're a good woman, Kathryn Templeton.'

Right then she would have given everything she possessed to have been able to tell him she loved him, that he could trust her, but it wasn't possible. All she could cling to was the fact that at least he had told her about his fiancée. It was something Agnes had said he never talked about. Maybe he had been driven to it by circumstances, but it was another tiny prop to shore up her heart.

Even as she held him, one tiny corner of her mind couldn't help wondering if she could be pregnant. As he had said, it was possible. A part of her hoped she was, for if she couldn't have him, at least she could have a part of him to love and care for. Yet it would change things. He hadn't mentioned marriage, and if he should suggest it could she go into it loving him as she did and knowing he would not allow himself to love her? That the marriage was only for the sake of the child? She honestly didn't know. She could only make that kind of decision if and when the time came.

'Now will you come back to bed?' she asked again, wanting to distract both Joel and herself from a subject that was too painful, and she felt the laugh rumble up from deep inside him.

'Are you sure you want me to?' he charged wryly, looking down at her.

'I don't have to get up for work, so I can catch up on my sleep later,' she told him impishly, and he grinned wolfishly.

'We aren't going to sleep?'

Kathryn held on to his robe as she allowed herself to sink back to the pillows. 'I'm not in the least bit tired. Are you?'

Joel followed her down, his lips hovering above hers. 'Now that you come to mention it…' he murmured, and kissed her.

Kathryn closed her eyes and kissed him back.

feel-follow of her dawn fall like towering above them. Now that your code termination til... be murmured, and kissed her.

Kath... to melt... inside them... held in their...

CHAPTER EIGHT

FOR Kathryn, the next few weeks passed in a blur. She was so happy she felt sure she wore a permanent smile on her face. They saw each other every day. Sometimes they went out, more often they stayed in, simply enjoying each other's company. To begin with Joel occasionally stayed over at her place, but as time went on more often than not they ended up at his house. Soon Kathryn took to leaving some clothes there, in case she had to go to an early meeting and there was no chance of going home first. Eventually, as more and more of her things ended up in his house, she was virtually living with him and only working from her own home.

Life was as close to idyllic as she could want it. The only small cloud on the horizon had been the recent discovery that she wasn't pregnant after all. When she'd told Joel, some emotion had flickered in his eyes. Relief? Regret? She couldn't be sure—it had gone too quickly for her to identify it. Nevertheless, their passion for each other had not diminished. In fact it had seemed to deepen, so that the more they made love, the stronger their need for each other became—although Joel never forgot to use protection. Her head knew he was right, but her heart wished it could have been otherwise, that he would one day want more from her. Even so, she kept telling him she loved him, although he was always asleep and never heard her.

Kathryn made a point of not looking ahead, but taking each day as it came. She knew she was living in a false sense of security. It was only a matter of time before her family discovered who she was seeing, and she knew that when that happened the full weight of family censure would fall on her head. Because they loved her, and they would feel there was no future for her with Joel. His reputation spoke for itself. Sometimes she felt as if she was holding her breath, waiting for the axe to fall.

It fell, as often happens, when it was least expected.

The telephone rang one Tuesday when Kathryn was working on a particularly complicated program for one of her new customers. She answered its persistent ring with an irritated sigh at having forgotten to switch the answering machine on, thus preventing this kind of interruption.

'Kathryn Templeton. How can I help you?'

'I can think of several ways you can help me, sweetheart, but they'd probably get us arrested,' Joel's sexy tones came down the line and curled her toes. Her irritation vanished like mist in sunlight.

Relaxing back against her chair, she laughed. 'Hmm, sounds interesting. What did you have in mind?'

'If I told you, you'd never get any work done this afternoon, and neither would I, so I think I'll save it till later,' he replied seductively, and Kathryn gave a tiny shiver of anticipation.

'I'll look forward to it. So, why are you calling?'

'Does there have to be a reason? Maybe I just like the sound of your voice,' he told her softly, and her heart skipped a beat.

'Do you? Like the sound of my voice?' she asked throatily. 'Because I can't tell you what yours is doing to me right now.'

'Let me tell you something, Kathryn,' Joel returned

confidentially. 'Your voice... Well, I'll just say that in certain circumstances, when I think of it, it can be downright distracting.'

Kathryn chuckled. 'Good. I like the sound of you being distracted.'

'I had a feeling you'd say that.'

'I try not to disappoint you,' she teased, and grinned when she heard him groan.

'This conversation is going to play merry hell with my afternoon. I don't know how I'm going to concentrate,' he murmured, with more than a hint of laughter in his voice.

Kathryn twined the telephone cord round her fingers and smiled up at the ceiling. 'I'd suggest a cold shower, but remembering what happened the last time you tried it...' She left the sentence hanging, and knew he was recalling yesterday morning, when she had joined him in the shower and, rather than cooling off, their temperatures had soared. One thing had led to another, and he had been late for work when he'd left the house.

'You'll pay for that, sweetheart,' he promised, and she laughed softly.

'I thought I already had, and I enjoyed every minute of it. You never did tell me what your secretary said when you finally got to your office.'

'She asked if I was unwell. I told her it was just temporary insanity. It's you I have to thank for the majority of my staff giving me very strange looks,' Joel complained. 'They don't say anything, but I know they think you're having a very deleterious effect on me.'

Her brows rose. 'I don't see why. I'm hardly the first woman in your life, nor the last.' As ever, she made a joke of it, but it wasn't getting any easier to say. She was in way too deep to escape from this unscathed, but it was a price she was willing to pay.

'No,' he agreed. 'But you are the first one who's ever made me late for work. Do you realise I've had to re-arrange more meetings in the last few weeks than in the last ten years?'

It was some comfort to know their relationship was different enough from the others to raise comment. 'Are you sorry?'

'The hell of it is, I'm not,' he told her, in a strange tone of voice which made her wish she could see him and read his expression. Right now it seemed important to know what he was really thinking. It was extremely frustrating to be on the end of a telephone line. 'Frankly, I'd rather be with you than in some stuffy boardroom, and that's not like me at all. Sometimes I think you must be a witch.'

'What kind of witch? The kind who turns you into a mouldy old toad, or the kind who puts a spell on you to bind you to her for ever?' Oh, if there only were such a spell! She'd use it quick as winking.

'The second one, naturally,' Joel came back, and she could hear his amusement.

Her smile faded, because she would give anything to believe he really felt more for her than just desire. It was no joke to her, yet she forced her voice to be light. 'And are *you* bound to *me* forever?' Say yes, her heart begged silently. Say yes.

'Of course. I'm your devoted slave,' Joel responded laconically, and her heart ached with disappointment. 'There isn't anything I wouldn't do for you,' he added, and it was salt to the wound, for the one thing she wanted he would never do. He would never give her his heart.

'Be careful, I just might hold you to that,' she warned through a tight throat, but he didn't appear to notice and merely laughed.

'Do you think that will make me renege?'

'Most men would.'

'I'm not most men. Haven't you figured that out for yourself? I'm made of stronger stuff. Try me.'

'I don't know, you'd probably wriggle out of it some-how,' she goaded.

'Now you malign my honour. I'm going to have to demand that you put me to the test,' Joel retorted, sounding very much on his dignity, though she didn't miss the smile in his voice.

Her own smile returned. 'OK, I will, but I'll have to think of something worthy. I'll get back to you on it.'

'Make it as difficult as you like,' he offered, and she grinned.

'Oh, believe me, I will. Now, are you going to tell me why you really called. Because if not, I've got work to do,' she charged him.

'You're a hard woman.'

Kathryn laughed. 'I'm going to put the phone down now,' she threatened sweetly.

'OK, you win. Slip yourself into something sexy and meet me here at seven tonight. I have a surprise for you. Don't be late,' he warned, and before she could get her wits together to respond he had rung off, and she was left staring at the receiver.

She returned it to the rest with a faint little sigh. Joel could be the most aggravating man, but Lord, how she loved him! Now she would be wondering all afternoon just what the surprise was, and he would know it. But she would pay him back. He had given her the oppor-tunity with that dare, and all she had to do was think up something really devilish. Having to fight four brothers all her life meant she had the best training to do it.

By seven that evening, Kathryn was riding up in the lift to the top floor of the modern office block that housed Joel's corporate headquarters. She had been here a few times before, and had been passed in with a smile and word of greeting by the security man on the door. The offices were empty as she walked the corridors to his office. His secretary had gone home long since, but the office door was ajar and she pushed it open quietly.

Joel was seated at a large desk, his head lowered as he studied some paperwork. As she watched he rolled his head to ease out the kinks before concentrating once more. A peculiar little lump lodged itself in her chest as she resisted the urge to go to him and simply hold him to take away the stresses and strains of the day. Yet she couldn't let it pass unremarked upon either.

'You work too hard,' she pronounced as she walked into the room, and Joel glanced up, a smile curving his lips and tweaking her heart. He closed the folder immediately and rose to come round and meet her.

'I have to make up the time I lost thinking of you during the day somehow,' he told her wryly, and pulled her into his arms. Kathryn raised her head to receive his kiss. It was languorous and deeply possessive, as if he were stamping his brand on her, and she wondered if he realised it. Not that it necessarily meant anything. He was probably the same way with all his women. Which reminded her unnecessarily that she only had him on a temporary basis.

A thought she resolutely blocked out as he raised his head and looked down at her, a possessive gleam in his eye. He allowed his gaze to rove over the discreet black dress she was wearing and nodded approvingly. 'Very nice.'

'Sexy enough?' she charged mockingly.

'You'd be sexy in a sack, but I've got to admit, less is definitely more,' he confided gruffly, referring to the fact that the dress showed very little bare flesh. 'My imagination can fill in the rest, and it's doing a grand job. Perhaps we ought to go home.'

'Oh, no!' Kathryn refused, placing her hands on his chest. 'Not before you give me the surprise you promised me.'

He sighed heavily. 'I suppose you're going to insist on it?'

'Absolutely. So give.'

Slipping an arm across her shoulders, he steered her to the door, switching off the light as he went. 'I just happen to have in my pocket tickets to the opening of the new Turner exhibition.'

Kathryn's head turned as if it were on a swivel. 'But I thought it was invitation only,' she exclaimed.

'It is, but I managed to wangle an invitation. However, we don't have to go if you'd rather not,' he teased, and she reached up quickly and kissed him.

'Thank you.' She adored Turner, and had been disappointed not to be able to go to the opening. She had said as much to Joel, and now he had conjured up tickets. Was it any wonder she loved him so much, when he did something thoughtful like that?

'Come along, we don't want to be late.' He urged her to the lift. 'You can thank me properly later.'

The exhibition was as wonderful as she had expected, and Kathryn wandered around on Joel's arm, a barely touched glass of white wine in her hand. She didn't notice the speculative looks she received from time to time, from people who recognised Joel and knew his reputation. Not until they literally bumped into an acquaintance of his who was clearly somewhat the worse for wear.

'Joel. Good to see you, old man,' he greeted effusively, with a public school accent, pumping Joel's hand as if he expected to get water out of it. 'What happened to the blonde I saw you with at Gstaad? Got to ask you, old chap. *Was* she more fun?' he queried with a loud laugh and a knowing wink.

Joel retrieved his hand with a faint grimace. 'You're drunk, Marcus, or you'd see I'm not alone,' he said with a haughtiness Kathryn had never heard before. Glancing up at him, she could see what the other man couldn't: a frostiness in his eyes which promised trouble.

'Oops, sorry. This the new filly?' Marcus carried on regardless, giving Kathryn the once over with a repulsive leer. 'She's a looker, but you always did manage to snap up the best ones.' He reached out a podgy hand towards Kathryn, but it was anyone's guess what he might have been going to do, for in flash Joel's hand had shot out and grasped the other man's wrist, holding it in a vice-like grip, preventing the move being completed.

'Keep your hands to yourself, Marcus,' he warned in a soft but deadly tone of voice that made the other man blink. 'You'd be well advised to go home and sleep this off.'

Kathryn thought it good advice as she glanced around uncomfortably. Thankfully, they were in a relatively quiet corner and the incident had gone unnoticed so far. Unfortunately, the man didn't take the hint.

'I'm not drunk, old chap, just well-lub-lubricated.' He grinned vacuously.

Joel's corresponding smile was grim. 'You're… lubricated…enough to insult this lady.'

Too far gone to exercise caution, Marcus snorted. 'Lady? When did you get to be so nice?' he charged as Kathryn's cheeks started to burn with embarrassed heat.

A nerve began to tick in Joel's jaw, so tight was he clenching it. 'Apologise, Marcus, or, so help me, I'll lay you out cold right here,' he threatened, and this time the message got through.

'OK, OK!' Marcus said hastily. 'I didn't realise I was stepping on your toes. I guess this one is special, eh?' He looked at Kathryn speculatively. 'I don't recall what I said, but I apologise if I upset you, Miss…?' He left that hanging, and Joel was quick to step in.

'Say goodnight, Marcus,' he urged, releasing the man's wrist. Marcus looked from one to the other, mumbled something which could have been goodnight, and hurried away.

Kathryn wasn't sorry to see him go. 'A friend of yours?' she asked sardonically, but Joel didn't smile.

'Not any longer,' he said coldly, and she glanced at him curiously as they strolled on.

'Would you really have hit him?' she couldn't help but ask.

'He was asking for it. People shouldn't drink if they can't hold their liquor,' Joel went on repressively, and Kathryn was left in a state of bemusement.

Nobody but her brothers had ever defended her so staunchly before, and they had a reason. She was their sister, and nobody was going to hurt her by word or by deed. She was nothing to Joel but a temporary lover, and yet he had come to her defence before she had even realised she was being offended. Her heart lurched. There was a name for that kind of response, and according to Joel the emotion didn't exist. It was a stunning thought. She wouldn't give it that name either, but could he *care* more for her than he was prepared to admit?

Now she came to think of it, there were many things he had said or done that, taken collectively, would seem to suggest that he more than cared for her. The trouble was, she had no way of knowing how much he had 'cared' for the other women he had had relationships with. So she had to be sensible and not get up false hopes, because even if he 'cared', that still didn't mean they had a future together.

Taking a breath to steady her pulse, she slipped her hand through Joel's arm. 'Well, thank you for defending me, though what he said didn't really bother me.'

'It bothered me,' Joel returned grittily, and that pleased her inordinately.

'Are you always this protective of your lady-friends?' she quipped lightly, though the answer held more importance for her than he would guess.

Joel paused before one large canvas and studied it so long she was sure he wasn't going to answer, but then he glanced down at her. 'I abhor men who speak of women like cattle. On the other hand, I don't think I've ever come so close to decking someone before. It would have given me great satisfaction to wipe the grin from his face.'

'I think he understood that eventually,' Kathryn murmured wryly.

'I didn't mean to embarrass you,' Joel apologised, running a gentle finger over her still flushed cheek.

She smiled up at him. 'You didn't embarrass me. I know it's probably old-fashioned, but it gave me a comfortable feeling, having a man come to my defence. I wouldn't want to give up my independence, but sometimes we women do appreciate the male protective instinct.'

Joel laughed, finally relaxing and losing that grim set to his mouth and eyes. 'You don't consider it too possessive, then.'

'It can be, in the wrong circumstances, but you don't come into that group. You protect women because it's what a man should do, simply because we cannot always defend ourselves. Speaking for myself, I like that in a man,' Kathryn responded honestly, then grinned at him. 'How's your ego doing?'

'Stroke it much more, and I'll be beating my chest like a gorilla. You certainly know how to make a man feel good,' Joel admitted, his eyes glinting with humour.

'Practice makes perfect. Not that I didn't mean what I said, but I have had to stroke a lot of male egos in my life.'

'Your brothers?'

Kathryn laughed. 'You got it,' she gurgled as they sauntered on again.

'Kathy?'

The sound of her name in an all too familiar voice had Kathryn tensing instantly. The moment she had been expecting any time these past weeks had arrived. Knowing who she would see, she pinned a determinedly cheery smile to her face as she turned.

'Hello, Nathaniel,' she greeted her brother, stepping forward to kiss his cheek.

'I thought it was you,' Nathaniel Templeton declared, returning the greeting. He was tall, sandy-haired, and built like a prop forward. 'I didn't expect to see you here.'

'Nor I you,' she said with a faint grimace. Joel had

turned, and she could sense him standing at her elbow, watching them. 'How are you?' she carried on, but her brother's attention had been caught by the man at her side. From the expression on his face, it was clear he recognised Joel, and didn't at all like finding his precious sister in the man's company. 'I suppose I'd better make the introductions. Joel, this is my brother Nathaniel. Nat, meet Joel Kendrick.'

Nathaniel reluctantly held out his hand. 'Kendrick,' he said curtly, which brought a faint smile to Joel's lips as he took the proffered hand.

'I'm pleased to meet you, Nathaniel. Kathryn's mentioned you several times. You play rugby, I believe?' he replied smoothly, with all the finesse she knew he was capable of. It would have disarmed a man made of less stern stuff than her brother.

'How long have you known my sister?' he demanded, point-blank, and Joel's brows rose as the gauntlet was well and truly thrown down.

'Several weeks now,' he informed him levelly, and Kathryn's heart sank at the look on her brother's face.

'I see.'

Joel smiled mockingly. 'Do you?'

Nathaniel chose not to respond to that, but instead turned to his sister. 'You've kept this very quiet.'

Her chin went up, and there was a warning light in her eye if he cared to note it. 'I happen to think a person's private life is precisely that—*private*.'

If she'd hoped that would rein him in, she was disappointed. Her brother ignored it and took her arm. 'Excuse us a moment,' he said to Joel, then drew her to one side. 'Are you crazy?' he demanded once they were out of earshot. 'Dad's going to blow a gasket when he finds out!'

Kathryn tugged her hand free, angry flags of colour burning her cheeks. 'Only if you tell him!' she whispered back angrily. 'This is none of your business, Nat, or Dad's.'

'Of course it is! That man's little better than a gigolo! What are you thinking of?'

That description of Joel turned her cheeks white with rage. 'Don't you ever call him that again, do you hear me?' she ordered, spitting mad, but Nathaniel had the hide of a rhinoceros.

'Are you sleeping with him?' he demanded to know next, and it made her so furious she was shaking with it.

'You have no right to ask that!'

'My God, you are!' he exclaimed in horrified disbelief.

Green eyes glittered with angry tears. She had known it was going to be like this! 'Whether I am or not is my business. Stay out of it.'

'You know I can't do that,' her brother said predictably, yet in a softer tone, his expression turning to one of concern. 'How can I simply close my eyes to this, when I know damn well you're making a terrible mistake?'

That was what she had always been afraid of. The cat was out of the bag, and her family cared for her too much to put it back again. She stiffened her spine and looked him in the eye.

'Then I guess you're going to have to do what you have to do. Don't expect me to thank you for it,' she told him stolidly, and, without another word, turned and walked away.

She walked past Joel, too, wanting to put some distance between herself and her brother, so didn't see the long, assessing look the two men exchanged before Joel came after her.

'Hey, where's the fire?' he teased lightly, though his eyes were watchful on her averted face.

Kathryn came to a standstill and sighed heavily. 'Sorry. I'm just…' She waved her hand for want of a word to describe exactly how she felt.

Placing his hands on her shoulders, Joel turned her to face him. 'What did he say to you?' he asked gently, tipping his head this way and that until he caught her eye, then holding her gaze resolutely. 'What did he say, Kathryn?'

'About what I expected,' she snapped. 'The game's up. As you know, he was appalled to see me with you. Quicker than you can say it, the whole family will know. You'll be able to hear the chorus of disapproval from the moon!'

'Hmm, I detected a definite frost in the air. I hope you told him to mind his own business?'

'I did, but I might as well have saved myself the trouble. He won't listen,' she replied glumly. A pall had come over the evening which had started so brightly.

'You're a grown woman, free to make your own choices.'

Kathryn laughed with scant humour. 'I'm his little sister and you're the Big Bad Wolf. If the roles were reversed, would you leave me in your clutches?' she asked him, and he frowned, then grimaced.

'Probably not,' he admitted wryly. 'So, what are you going to do?'

'Nothing. I'm certainly not about to give you up!' Kathryn declared forcefully, bringing a smile to his lips.

'You're not, eh?'

Tipping her head up, Kathryn smiled defiantly. 'Stubbornness runs in the family. Nobody can make me do anything I don't want to do. I knew what I was taking on by getting involved with you, Joel. I knew my family would cry foul. But I was prepared for that because I wanted to be with you.'

That confession brought a faint frown to his forehead. 'It isn't going to be easy, is it?'

Her smile grew rueful. 'I thought I'd have more time with you before the flak started to fly.'

'Perhaps we should call it quits, Kathryn. I'm not worth alienating your family over,' he told her with unfamiliar sombreness, and her heart lodged in her throat.

'Do you want me to go?' she challenged him, and after a significant pause Joel shook his head.

'I suppose I ought to do the decent thing, but I'm not ready to end this yet. I want you too damned much.'

Kathryn's lips curved into a wide smile. 'Then I'll stay.'

'It's as simple as that?'

'Of course. I'm a simple woman. I know what I want, and I'm willing to pay the price for it. My family will be upset, but it won't last.' How true that was. When this affair was over, and she was hurting as they would no doubt expect her to be, then they would be the first to rally round to comfort her.

Joel shook his head, as if he didn't understand her at all. 'You're an extraordinary woman.'

She laughed that off. 'I'm not extraordinary at all.' She was simply a woman who loved him. 'And don't imagine you're going to get off lightly. Pressure will be brought to bear. Just wait and see.'

'I think I can handle your family,' Joel said confidently, and she wasn't about to disabuse him. He would find out that the Templeton clan, separately and together, made a formidable fighting machine.

'Right,' she agreed dryly.

'I'm not about to give you up without a fight either.'

She laughed. 'That, I can safely say, you will get. It won't be pretty. In fact, it will get downright dirty. Do you think I'm worth it? You could cut and run to the next woman down the line, you know.' Though she made light of it, it was all too true. It would be oh, so easy for him to walk away.

'I could, but right now the only woman I can see is you. You're the only woman I want in my life, so I guess I'll just have to take my chances with your family.'

'I guess we're stuck with each other, then.'

'Looks like it,' Joel agreed.

Suddenly Kathryn wished they were somewhere else. Somewhere she could kiss him and not cause a minor scandal. 'I don't know about you, but I think I've had enough art for one evening.'

'I couldn't agree more,' Joel concurred, turning them towards the archway that would eventually take them to the entrance. 'Do you want to go somewhere for dinner?'

'To tell you the truth, I'd much rather go home. We can order something in if we're hungry,' Kathryn declared, and the look he gave her held a decided glint.

'Or, if we're not, I'm sure we can think of something to do to pass the time,' he drawled seductively, setting her nerves alight.

'Just what I was thinking myself,' she said with a grin.

Outside the gallery, Joel hailed a passing taxi and

gave the driver his address. She didn't argue. Wherever he was, was where she wanted to be. Maybe her time with Joel was going to be short, but one thing she did know: it was never going to be dull.

CHAPTER NINE

KATHRYN was in her kitchen preparing dinner on Thursday evening when she heard the front door shut with some force. Her eyes widened in surprise. She knew it was Joel, for she had arranged for him to come to her house tonight. She had had to travel for a consultation, and so had decided to cook dinner here for a change. Her surprise came from his being so early—almost an hour before he was expected—and, for another thing, he had not come straight through to find her and kiss her as he usually did.

Popping the salad she had been tossing back into the refrigerator, she wiped her hands on a towel and went off in search of him. Joel was in her sitting room in the process of pouring himself a drink. As she watched, he downed half of it in one go, giving every impression that he had really needed it. He studied the remaining half of the golden liquid broodingly.

'Bad day?' she queried consolingly, and he glanced round, for once not smiling when he saw her.

'A hell of a bad day,' he confirmed with a grimace, using his free hand to loosen his tie and unfasten the top buttons of his shirt. The jacket of his suit was draped haphazardly over a chair, looking for all the world as if it had been tossed there.

Kathryn went into the room and retrieved his jacket, laying it out properly so it didn't crease. 'Care to talk about it?' she offered, going to him and deftly removing the tie altogether.

'I'm just about all talked out,' he said tiredly, flexing his shoulders as if they were still tense.

'Difficult meeting?' she tried again, feeling as if she was attempting to get blood out of a stone.

His laugh was wry. 'Several difficult meetings,' he revealed with a heavy sigh. 'You warned me, so it's my own fault for not taking it seriously enough. You're quite within your rights to say I told you so.'

Light dawned. 'Oh, no!' she groaned.

'Oh, yes,' Joel confirmed sardonically, finishing his drink and setting the glass aside.

The meetings Joel had had, had been with her brothers. She had expected it—the only surprise being that they had waited until today.

She sought clarification with a sinking heart. 'Which ones?'

'All of them.' He grimaced, then shook his head and laughed. 'My God, they were good. They could grill for England.'

'Lord, I'm sorry,' Kathryn apologised, thinking she would have a word or two to say herself when she ran into the four of them again.

Joel, perversely, had started to relax. Taking her hand, he dropped down into a chair and pulled her onto his lap. 'Hell, don't be. They were there because they care about you, and that's something I approve of—though, given a choice, I'd rather not have been on the receiving end of it.'

'What did they say?' she asked curiously.

Unconsciously, Joel's hand began to run caressingly along her stocking-clad thigh. 'First they suggested I get out of your life. When I said I couldn't do that, they demanded to know what my intentions were. Which, as I told them, is my business. We circled around that for a while, then they told me what they would do to me if I should hurt you. The methods of my demise were inventive, to say the least.'

Kathryn had gone from dismay to seething by this time. 'Oh, I could strangle all of them!'

'Janet thought it was highly amusing,' he went on, referring to his secretary. 'She wasn't eavesdropping, but the walls are thin and voices were raised. She thinks it's long past time I got my comeuppance. I have to admit, the Templeton boys are just the men to do it, too.'

She frowned at him in perplexity, for, on the whole, he was taking this very well. 'How can you laugh about it?'

'Because they all wanted to grind my face into the dirt. I liked them,' Joel admitted, surprising her.

'Well, I hate them!' she snapped, so angry she could spit nails. Why couldn't they just leave well enough alone?

'No, you don't,' Joel corrected immediately. 'You love them as much as they love you.'

'Maybe I do,' she retorted in a disgruntled tone. 'I just wish they'd stop interfering in my life.' They had no idea what they were doing. OK, Joel had taken it well so far, but he had to draw the line somewhere, and what if they pushed him over it? How much longer would he consider their affair worth it with four angry men breathing fire down his neck? Damn them, they could ruin everything and bring about what they were trying to avoid.

'Trust me, it will never happen. You'll always be their little sister. They'll always look out for you. Try to protect you from the Big Bad Wolves of this world.'

'Whilst I accept that, they have to be made to understand that I don't need protecting from you,' Kathryn insisted, frowning heavily. There was a sinking feeling in her stomach that time was running out.

Joel cupped his hand about her cheek and turned her head until she was looking at him. 'Do you want to know what the really crazy thing is?' he asked with a self-mocking smile. 'I don't want to see you get hurt either.'

'Don't be silly.' She rushed to reassure him. 'You won't hurt me.'

Rather than smiling, Joel's expression was sober as he looked deeply into her eyes. 'Won't I? I'm beginning to wonder. For one thing, sweetheart, you're nowhere near as hard-boiled as you'd like me to believe.'

She tensed immediately, alarm signals going off in her head. 'What are you suggesting?' she asked uneasily. If he had somehow guessed her secret...

'Only that if everyone is doing their best to ensure you won't get hurt, then that means you can be. I'd hate to be the cause of it. Maybe your brothers are right. Maybe I should get out of your life,' he mused broodingly, and Kathryn's body felt a jolt of panic.

'Don't you dare walk out on me, Joel Kendrick. I'd never forgive you,' she declared hotly.

He frowned at her vehemence. 'I'm thinking of you, Kathryn. What would be best for you. I'm bad news.'

'Not to me you're not!' she insisted, and he smiled faintly.

'You shouldn't try and stop me doing the right thing. I haven't had such a noble feeling in years.'

She sniffed. 'Personally, I think nobility is highly overrated.' Especially if it meant she could lose him.

'All the same,' he went on with a sigh, 'I don't know

how long I can continue to keep you away from the press.'

Her brows rose. 'You mean you have something to do with the fact I haven't had my picture splashed across the tabloids?' She had been relieved to discover her presence in Joel's life wasn't news, but puzzled all the same. Now she knew why.

Blue eyes quartered her face, as if he was memorising it. 'I found I had a dislike of the idea of seeing you in print under some sensation-seeking banner. So far as I'm concerned, you're not for public consumption. I have no intention of sharing you with half the country, so I've simply been exercising more discretion.'

Kathryn's lips parted on a tiny gasp of surprise, even as her heart swelled with pleasure. There it was again, that caring he professed not to have any time for. He didn't want to see her hurt, and he didn't want her the subject of general gossip. That had to mean something, didn't it? Deep down inside, he had to care, didn't he? Lord, how she wished she knew for sure. Hiding her feelings was so unnatural. She wanted to reach out to him, show him how much she cared. It was getting harder to hold back all the time.

Swallowing a lump that blocked her throat, she smiled. 'Thank you. That was very thoughtful.'

'You're welcome, but it was entirely selfish. I don't want to share you. I want to keep you all to myself.'

That declaration warmed her heart, and Kathryn guarded it jealously as she combed her fingers through his hair, enjoying the silky texture. 'Well, I have no problem with that,' she said softly. 'I want you all to myself, too.'

Joel caught her hand and pressed a kiss to her palm.

'I've never known anyone like you. You make no demands. Isn't there anything you want?'

Her heart ached. She wanted so many things she couldn't name them all. But, in the long run, her happiness boiled down to one thing alone. Him. 'Well, now you come to mention it, I could do with your help opening a bottle of wine,' she said teasingly, loving the way laughter softened his face.

'Now, that is something I can do,' he declared, coming to his feet in one smooth movement with her still in his arms. Only in the kitchen did he lower her to the ground, tantalisingly allowing her body to slide down the length of his as he did so.

Kathryn looked up at him, her eyes twinkling. 'Hmm, your mood seems to have changed for the better,' she teased saucily, having felt his body respond to her as quickly as hers did to him.

'The things you do to me!' Joel grinned and gently pushed her away. 'I'd better see to the wine before you distract me too much.'

Laughing, she turned to the cooker. 'You can lay the table whilst you're about it. That should cool your ardour.'

'Don't you believe it, sweetheart,' he retorted as he retrieved the bottle from the refrigerator. 'Just being in the same room as you turns me on. I thought it would have lessened by now, but the more I see of you, the more I want. I'm addicted.'

She halted in the process of unwrapping some steak. 'Is that a good thing or a bad thing?'

'Oh, good. Definitely good. I usually get bored easily, but you're never boring, Kathryn. In fact, you're constantly surprising me.'

'I like keeping you on your toes. I wouldn't want our

relationship to grow stale,' she returned, concentrating on what she was cooking.

Joel set the opened bottle of wine on the table and came across to collect the cutlery. 'It will never get stale,' he told her, and she felt her smile fade. Without looking at him, she corrected him.

'Yes, it will. One day.'

He glanced sideways at her, frowning. 'Why do you say that?' he asked, and she did look at him now, her lips twisting wryly.

'Because my successor is out there somewhere, waiting to catch your eye,' she told him simply.

Joel stared at her, his frown deepening. Something flickered in the far reaches of his eyes, but she didn't know how to interpret it. Then he was turning away, setting places at the table.

'I wasn't thinking that far ahead,' he said uncomfortably, which was so unlike him she had to turn and watch him. 'I'm just happy that you're here now.'

'Are you?'

He glanced up. 'Of course. There isn't anyone else I want to be with right now.'

'But you can't rule out the possibility that that will change in the future?' she charged, being urged on by her feelings for him.

'No, I can't do that. Why are you asking me this now, Kathryn?' he probed, eyes narrowing on her face.

'I guess I just need to know where I stand.' She shrugged, smiling wryly.

Joel put down the cutlery and came across to her, taking her by the shoulders and giving her a gentle shake. 'We're together now, and I'm happy with that. I thought you were, too.'

'I am,' she insisted, quick to reassure him. 'I'm just

being fanciful. Forget I mentioned it. Let me get these steaks on, or we won't be eating until midnight.' She twisted out of his hold and busily set about collecting a frying pan and olive oil. She could sense Joel watching her, but she refused to turn around. Eventually he returned to the table.

Nothing more was said, and it was forgotten when they sat down to eat the meal she had prepared. She told him about her day, and he related more of his runins with her brothers, but in such a way that she was more amused than angry.

She was still laughing when the front doorbell rang. They were washing up, and she paused in the act of drying a plate. Surprised, she glanced up at the clock. It was almost ten o'clock.

'Who on earth can that be?' She frowned, setting the plate and tea towel aside, then heading for the door.

The man standing on her doorstep when she opened the door could have been one of her brothers, except for his greying hair.

'Dad!' Kathryn exclaimed in equal amounts of surprise and dismay. 'This is a surprise! What brings you here?' she added lamely, and wasn't surprised by the old-fashioned look he graced her with.

'Are you going to invite me in?' Victor Templeton prompted his daughter, and she stepped back, casting a weather eye towards the kitchen, but there was no sign of Joel.

'Of course. Come in.' She left him to close the door and led the way into the sitting room. There she turned, rather like a stag at bay, nervously rubbing her hands together. 'Er…sit down, won't you? Would you like a drink?'

Her father cut through all the polite inanities and

came right to the point. 'What's this I hear about you and that Kendrick fellow?'

Her back went up immediately at that, and her nervousness vanished as she folded her arms belligerently. 'His name is Joel, and what exactly did you want to know?' She hadn't been looking forward to this meeting with her father, but now that the moment was here she was prepared to do battle.

Red flags of colour stained his lined cheeks at her reply. 'So you are going out with him.'

'I'm sure Nat and the others have already told you so. What you really want to know is if I'm sleeping with him, and the answer to that is yes, I am,' she told him with a defiant lift of her chin.

Victor Templeton took in an angry breath. 'Don't get lippy with me, Kathryn. I'm still your father.'

Kathryn sighed at the unnecessary reminder. 'I know you are, and I love you, but you have no right to try to interfere in my life, Dad,' she told him, as she had told her brother.

'I wouldn't call concern interfering,' he argued, closing the distance between them, and she could see the concern written on his face.

'You mean you have no intention of trying to break us up?' she countered chidingly, and her father ground his teeth impotently, for, as they both knew, that was what he had intended.

He tried another tack. 'I know you, Kathryn. You would never go into a relationship unless you cared for the man, which does you credit, but in this case he's unworthy of you.'

'I disagree. He is worthy; you just don't know him. He's a good man, Dad,' she retorted, staunchly defensive.

'I know you think so, but he's what we used to call a philanderer, a playboy,' he returned forcefully. 'He's just toying with your affections. He won't marry you, you know.'

If he'd hoped to unsettle her with that, he failed. 'I'm fully aware of that,' she said evenly, and his eyes widened.

'Doesn't that bother you?'

Kathryn sighed again, then lowered her voice and motioned her father to do the same. 'I'd be lying if I said it didn't. Of course I want to marry him. I love him. I want to spend my life with him, have children with him. But I have to be practical. That isn't what he wants. I know this is just another affair to him, and maybe it does hurt to know that, but if that's all he can give, I'll take it.'

He father stared at her in consternation. 'Can you hear yourself? Don't you have any pride?'

Kathryn disliked disappointing him this way, but it was her life, her decision. She held his gaze stoically. 'Apparently not.'

'Does he love you?'

It was a calculatingly cruel question, and she felt it to her soul. Nevertheless, she answered honestly, for there was no point in lying. 'No. I think he cares about me, but no, he doesn't love me.' She didn't tell him that Joel didn't believe love existed.

'Damn it, that makes no sense! If he doesn't love you, Kathryn, why put yourself through this?' Victor asked in a softer, more cajoling tone.

'I told you. Because I love him, Dad, that's why.'

Her father raised his hands helplessly, then dropped them to his sides with a shake of his head. 'Does he know you love him?'

She shook her head. 'No.'

He dragged both hands through his hair in a gesture she recognised well. 'If I can't persuade you to see sense, just remember you know where we are when you need us.'

She had known he would say that in the end, and it brought a lump to her throat. 'Thanks for caring so much. I'm sorry if I've disappointed you.'

'You could never disappoint me, Kathryn. I realise this is your life, and I have to let you live it, but it isn't easy to let go, not when I can see you heading for disaster. Is he really worth it?'

'I think so,' she declared with a reassuring smile, which made him sigh and hold out his arms.

'Come and give me a hug, then,' he ordered gruffly, and, crossing the room, Kathryn slipped into his arms, feeling comforted, as she had when she was a child.

A noise at the doorway made them both turn in that direction. Joel stood there, his expression enquiring. He looked from her to her father and back again. Her heart lurched, as she wondered if he had overheard anything, despite their efforts to speak softly.

'Kathryn? Is everything all right?' he asked smoothly as he came into the room.

He was too bland, she decided. He had to have heard something. Easing away from her father, she took her cue from Joel and smiled and nodded. 'Perfectly. My father called round unexpectedly,' she explained, her eyes searching his. But he was giving nothing away.

He turned to her father with an easy smile and held out his hand. 'Good evening, Mr Templeton. I'm sure you know who I am,' he greeted, with more than a hint of irony.

'Your fame goes before you, Mr Kendrick,' Victor

Templeton returned with heavy meaning, nevertheless shaking the proffered hand.

Joel's smile broadened. 'Yes. I had the pleasure of meeting your sons earlier.'

'They're very protective of their sister,' her father confided unnecessarily. 'Woe betide anyone who does her harm.'

Joel inclined his head, then looked squarely at the older man. 'I have no intention of harming your daughter, sir.'

'That may be, young man, but the road to hell is paved with good intentions,' Victor pronounced portentously, and Joel winced.

'The trouble with having a reputation like mine is that nobody believes I could have good intentions,' he returned wryly, and Kathryn's father harrumphed.

'Probably because you've gone out of your way to prove the opposite. But I take your point and promise you this. By my family you will be judged by your actions now. My daughter believes you're a good man, don't prove her wrong,' Victor Templeton warned, before turning to his daughter and kissing her cheek. 'I'll say goodnight now, Kathryn. Remember what I said.' He gave Joel one last pointed look, then marched from the room.

'I'll see you out, Dad,' Kathryn said, following him to the door. There her father squeezed her arm comfortingly.

'I hope for your sake he does prove me wrong,' he said, before striding down the path to his car.

Kathryn closed the door with a sense of fatalism. If she was right, the cat was well and truly out of the bag, and there was nothing she could do about it. The ball was in Joel's court. She returned to the sitting room, feeling calmer than she had expected to. Joel was standing by the fireplace, head lowered, gaze fixed on the empty grate. He straightened as she entered, his hands slipping into his trouser pockets as he watched her consideringly.

Halting several feet away from him, she took the bull by the horns. 'How long had you been standing out there?' she asked, though in her mind it was a foregone conclusion.

'Long enough,' he said coolly, and she nodded wryly.

'You know, then.' It was a statement, not a question.

'That you love me? Yes,' he confirmed, without even the faintest flicker of emotion. They could have been discussing the weather for all the interest he showed.

Kathryn grimaced inwardly. Had she been hoping for a miraculous declaration of similar feelings, she would have been disappointed. She was too sensible for that, but his apparent indifference did hurt. He could at least have been angry, she thought irritably.

In response her chin went up a notch. 'You weren't meant to hear any of that. Do you make a habit of listening at keyholes?'

That did get a response. A nerve started ticking in his jaw. 'When you didn't come back I thought the caller might be one of your brothers and that you might need moral support. When I realised it was your father, I hesitated,' Joel confessed tightly, and she smiled grimly.

'And consequently heard more than you'd bargained for!' she jibed.

Blue eyes locked with green. 'Is it true? Did you mean it?'

She held his gaze unflinchingly. 'It isn't something I

would lie about. I do love you.' For all the good it does
me.

It was Joel who looked away for a second, dragging
a hand through his hair before sighing and looking at
her again. 'You hid it well.'

Kathryn laughed. 'Well, I'm hardly going to wear my
heart on my sleeve, am I? Not when I know you don't
want to know,' she told him pointedly. 'And, as you
still don't want to know, I suggest you just forget about
it. I don't know about you, but I could do with some
coffee. I'll set it filtering whilst we finish the washing
up,' she went on matter-of-factly, turning on her heel
and walking back to the kitchen.

It wasn't easy to act so blasé, but she had no choice.
She was absolutely not going to have him pity her. No
way would she be able to bear that.

Kathryn was spooning coffee into the filter when Joel
caught up with her. Taking her by the shoulder, he spun
her round so fast she dropped the packet. When she met
his eyes they were no longer cool, but there was a blaze
in their depths that set her heart tripping.

'How can you be so damned cool about it?' he demanded, with all the emotion she could have hoped for.

With a swift gesture she brushed his hand away. 'Because beating my breast and tearing my hair out would
be a waste of time. I'm being ''cool'' because I have
no choice,' she told him as she hunkered down to retrieve what she could of the coffee.

Joel instantly hauled her back up again. 'What do you
mean, you have no choice?' he charged, taking the coffee packet from her and tossing it onto the counter top,
where it spilled out again.

Ignoring the coffee, Kathryn turned to the sink,
picked up the tea towel and began drying dishes. 'I have

no choice because nothing has changed, has it?' she threw over her shoulder.

Impatiently Joel took the cloth and dish from her, set them aside with a clatter that made her wince for her crockery, and almost frog-marched her to a chair, where he exerted enough downward pressure to make her sit.

'Leave the blasted dishes alone!' he commanded, pulling out a chair and sitting so close she would have had difficulty rising had she wanted to. 'Get to the point, Kathryn.'

'Very well,' she agreed. 'You didn't love me before, did you?' she challenged, and he sat back, eyes narrowing.

'No,' he confirmed shortly.

Her heart was racing uncomfortably fast, but she persisted. 'And you don't love me now, do you?'

Joel's head went back, and there was the faintest of hesitations before he said what she had known he would. 'No, I don't.'

No more than she had expected, but difficult to take all the same. She had to swallow hard to continue. 'So nothing has changed. Life goes on. You just know something you didn't know before. But, hey, it isn't going to kill you,' she jibed.

Joel's eyes narrowed to angry slits. 'And just how in hell am I supposed to forget what you said?'

Kathryn raised her eyebrows at that. 'I should imagine it would be easy if it isn't important to you,' she told him evenly, and whatever he had been about to say got lost in the shuffle.

That nerve began to tick again as he stared at her. 'Damn it, Kathryn, I warned you not to fall for me!' he exclaimed angrily, shooting to his feet and striding to the back door, which he opened, then stared out into the night, taking in deep breaths of the cold air.

Kathryn watched him, scarcely knowing what to make of this remarkable display. He had never shown so much emotion before. 'Why are you so angry? This is my problem, not yours,' she said simply. 'I'm not asking you to love me back.' Even though I want you to, so very, very badly.

He turned and looked at her through stormy blue eyes. 'How could you do something so stupid as to fall in love with me, Kathryn? After all I said.'

She couldn't help but smile. 'I couldn't help it. I told you, people don't choose to fall in love, they just do. That's what happened to me.'

Joel shook his head. 'You're forcing me to hurt you.'

'I don't blame you for that. It was inevitable from the moment I realised how I felt about you. But you don't have to worry, I'm prepared to take the consequences.'

His fist hit the doorframe, making her jump. 'Well, I sure as hell am not!'

She wondered if he realised how revealing that statement was. 'Would it hurt you to hurt me?' she asked in a rather strained voice, for the answer was important.

'Of course it would!' he shot back instantly, but there was no 'of course' about it for her. He gave so little away she had to scrabble for crumbs.

Her smile was rueful. 'So you care for me a little, then?'

That brought him up short, and he blinked at her as the import of the question sank in. Then he frowned. 'I care for you a lot. That's why I don't want to see you hurt, Kathryn,' he told her huskily and her heart turned over. It meant so much to her to hear him say that.

A wistful smile curved her lips. 'I'm afraid that can't be avoided now. No matter what you do. You have to decide where we go from here. As I see it, you have two choices. End it now, or later.'

Joel stared at her sombrely, clearly deep in thought. For a while she didn't think he was going to answer at all. When he did speak, what he had to say was totally unexpected.

'There is a third option,' he said slowly, clearly churning over the ramifications in his mind. 'We could get married.'

Kathryn's heart crashed against the wall of her chest as if trying to get out. Marriage? The possibility had only presented itself to her as a sort of last resort, in case she'd been pregnant—but they both knew that wasn't the case. That he would consider it as an option now stunned her.

'You can't be serious!' she exclaimed breathlessly.

'Why not?' He shrugged. 'I always intended to get married one day.'

Kathryn shook her head to try and clear it. 'Are you seriously suggesting that you could marry me in order not to hurt me?' she asked carefully, because it was the craziest thing she had ever heard. Of all the reasons to get married, that had to be at the bottom of the list.

'Don't you want to marry me?' Joel countered. 'Don't you want to marry the man you say you love?'

Her lips parted on a tiny gasp. Of course she wanted to marry him, but not like this. It was too bizarre. 'You don't really want to marry me. You don't love me,' she pointed out shakily.

'I care for you more than any other woman I know. We have a lot in common. The more I think about it, marriage to you makes sense,' he told her firmly.

Kathryn shook her head dazedly several times and pressed a hand to her forehead. 'You are serious.'

He nodded decisively. 'Never more so.'

'But you don't believe in love,' she exclaimed in confusion.

'I don't have to love you to marry you. I've told you that before. What I can promise you, if you agree to marry me, is to make sure you never regret doing so. I will honour our vows and be faithful to them. Think about it, Kathryn. Wouldn't it solve everything?' Joel urged, coming to her and squatting down, taking her chilly hands in his.

She searched his eyes, and realised with a sense of awe that he was sincere. She could have him for always. All she had to do was say yes.

'You know this is crazy,' she whispered, and he grinned, twisting her heart.

'Sometimes crazy is the only way to be,' he reminded her.

Kathryn licked her lips. 'If I agree, don't expect me to hide how I feel. I couldn't do that. It's been hard enough up to now. If I marry you, it will be because I love you, and I will make sure you know it. Could you live with that?'

'So long as you don't expect it to change anything,' he agreed, laying down the parameters of their relationship. 'Well?' he prompted.

'Don't I have time to think about it?'

'How much time do you need? What will you know in an hour that you don't know now? Either you want to marry me or you don't.'

He was right, damn it. She was just procrastinating. He was offering her more than she could ever have expected. He cared about her; she believed that. One day that caring might turn to love, but it would mean taking a gamble on her part now, with no guarantee for the future. Could she do it?

Kathryn drew in a deep breath and took that leap of faith. 'Yes, I'll marry you, Joel,' she accepted, knowing there was no way back now. There was no shame in trying and failing. If all she ever had was what she had now, it would be enough. She would make it enough.

Something like relief flickered in his eyes for a moment, then was gone, and she told herself she must have been imagining things. What reason did he have for being relieved?

'I promise you, you won't regret it,' he told her again as he stood and pulled her into his arms, holding her close.

Kathryn held on tight. She hoped not. Oh, Lord, she surely hoped not, she prayed.

CHAPTER TEN

THERE were times the following day that Kathryn felt as if she was living in a dream. She kept pinching herself to see if she was awake. Nothing seemed quite real, even when Joel took her to a high-class jeweller's so she could pick out her engagement ring—a gorgeous solitaire diamond. Yet she could not doubt his commitment, for at the same time he insisted on buying matching wedding bands. All the same, she couldn't help feeling that she would wake up soon and discover it had all been a dream.

The feeling persisted until Saturday morning, then vanished when her mother telephoned whilst they were eating a late breakfast at her place.

'Kathryn, darling, I'm so happy for you. I forgive you for keeping me totally in the dark!' Lucy Templeton declared as soon as she heard her daughter's voice.

Kathryn's jaw dropped in surprise. 'Mother, I don't—'

'Is he handsome? Do you love him? Lord, what a stupid question. Of course you love him! Tell me all about him. I'm dying to know everything,' her mother went on with scarcely a pause for breath.

Slowly, Kathryn turned to look at Joel, who was watching her over the top of the newspaper. 'Yes, he is handsome, Mother. At least, I think so. And, yes, I love him very much,' she responded when she could get a word in.

'Have you set a date yet? Is it to be a church wedding?' Lucy bubbled with questions, but they only served to puzzle her daughter more.

'Nothing's set yet. Er…how did you find out about it?' Superstitiously, she had said nothing to anyone, not even her family. Now it appeared they knew.

'Why, the engagement notice is in all the papers. I've had calls from friends and family since first thing. It was a little odd not to have any details to tell them, for I was just as surprised to hear about your engagement myself. However, I waffled. Darling, you must bring him to lunch tomorrow. I'm dying to meet him in the flesh. Your father tells me he's very well respected in the City. Is he there? Can I talk to him?'

'Just a second.' Kathryn halted the flow and held out the receiver. 'My mother would like a word with you.'

Joel came and took it from her and she left him chatting to her mother whilst she checked out the newspaper. The notice was there all right. Kathryn Templeton was engaged to Joel Kendrick. The feeling of unreality vanished like morning mist. This was no dream; this was really happening. Joel had asked her to marry him and she had agreed. Now it was official.

'I'm afraid lunch is out of the question. Kathryn and I have somewhere to go in the morning. Could you make it dinner? And would it be all right if I brought a guest?'

Kathryn glanced round quickly when she heard that. She looked a question, but Joel shook his head. A minute or two later he put the phone down.

'A nice woman, your mother,' he pronounced, strolling back to the table.

'I think so,' Kathryn agreed, frowning. 'Where do we have to go tomorrow, and why didn't you tell me about the notice?'

Joel grinned unrepentantly. 'I thought it would be a nice surprise. Besides, it was the quickest way of telling the greatest number of people in the shortest space of time.'

It was certainly a surprise, she thought dryly. 'And tomorrow?'

'Ah, that's a surprise too,' he said mysteriously, and refused to be pumped for any information.

'I hate surprises!' Kathryn exclaimed at last, and Joel laughed.

'No, you don't. Anyway, even if you do, you'll like this one.'

'How can you be so sure?' she demanded grumpily. 'I could hate it.'

'Trust me?' he suggested, keeping frustratingly mum.

Her eyes narrowed on his averted profile. 'How can I trust a man who didn't even tell me he'd put the notice of our engagement in the papers?'

His head turned and blue eyes locked on hers. 'Because you love me,' he said simply, and that took the wind out of her sails completely.

'That was a low blow, Kendrick!' she accused, stabbing a finger at him. 'I don't think I love you after all.'

'You will, tomorrow,' Joel returned confidently, neatly folding the newspaper and setting it down on the table. His smile appeared briefly. 'Trust me,' he added, and Kathryn rolled her eyes.

'You are the most...grr!' she finished, flinging up her hands helplessly.

'So, where do you want to go for your honeymoon?' he asked next, making her frown.

'Why are you going to all this trouble, Joel? You can't possibly want all this fuss!' she challenged, not understanding him at all.

'Because both of us intend getting married only once, and in that case we're going to do it right.'

He stunned her with his answer. She had expected he would insist on the rather clinical atmosphere of a register office.

'But it's all so romantic, and…you don't love me,' she argued gruffly.

Joel's eyes fell away from hers, and he reached across to take her hand, locking his fingers with hers. 'I assumed you would want a white wedding. Am I wrong?' When he looked up at her again, he was frowning.

Kathryn instantly felt guilty. He was doing all this for her, because he thought it was what she wanted, and he wanted to make her happy. 'You're right, I do want a white wedding. I thought it was out of the question because our marriage…' She cut off the rest of the sentence, but Joel finished it for her.

'Isn't real? You're wrong, you know. It's going to be very real. Which is why we have to do it right. So, a white wedding it shall be, and then the honeymoon. If you ever tell me where you want to go,' he teased, and her heart swelled, because she loved him all the more for doing this when he didn't have to.

'Oh, I don't know,' Kathryn declared with a shrug, then grinned. 'Surprise me.'

'But you don't like surprises,' he reminded her, and she laughed aloud.

'I lied.'

'Hmm, I see I'm going to have my work cut out with you, sweetheart,' Joel growled, tugging at her hand until he had pulled her up from her chair and onto his lap.

Kathryn smiled down into his eyes. 'I never said I was going to make it easy,' she taunted softly.

He grinned back, his teeth flashing whitely. 'I wouldn't want it any other way.'

Cupping her free hand to his cheek, Kathryn dropped a kiss on his nose. 'I love you,' she said huskily.

Joel's expression was serious as he looked deeply into her eyes. 'I know you do, Kathryn. I won't forget it.'

'See you don't,' she cautioned as the telephone shrilled out once more. 'Something tells me this is going to go on all day,' she groaned as she stood up. 'Your turn.'

'What if it's one of your brothers?' Joel charged and she grinned at him.

'Don't worry, they won't be after your blood now. After all, you're going to make an honest woman of me. That has to be worth several hundred Brownie points.'

'Hmm,' Joel responded. 'That may be, but I was in the Boy Scouts.'

Kathryn started to laugh. 'I bet you looked really sweet in uniform. All gangly and knobbly-kneed.'

'I looked better in my birthday suit.' He grinned, lifting the receiver.

'Take it from me, darling, you still do.'

Joel was about to respond to that when the person at the other end of the line demanded his attention. His eyes promising retribution, he turned and gave his full attention to the caller. Kathryn smiled and began clearing the breakfast things. It was going to be all right. They would make the marriage work because they cared about each other. So what if he didn't love her? She had enough love for the two of them. Besides, one day… But that was only wishful thinking. Sighing, she carried the dishes to the sink and turned on the tap.

*   *   *

By half past ten the following morning they were in Joel's car, heading north out of the City.

'Where are we going?' Kathryn asked as Joel threaded his way through the Sunday morning traffic, which could sometimes be as heavy as a week day. 'Or is that a secret, too?'

'Cambridge,' he told her concisely, and her brows rose.

'Cambridge? Why Cambridge?' So far as she could recall, she had never been there in her life.

'You'll see when we get there,' he told her with infuriating lack of information.

'I'm surprised somebody hasn't strangled you before now,' Kathryn grumbled, though not really seriously. Folding her coat around her, she sat back to enjoy the ride. Joel cast her a sideways look and bit back a smile.

In a very short space of time they reached the beautiful Fenland town. Joel stopped once to study some directions he had been given, then drove on past the architectural wonders of the university colleges. Eventually they left the pale stone buildings behind and entered a residential area. Kathryn was no more the wiser as to why they were here when Joel pulled up before a well-kept bungalow that looked in no way remarkable from all the others around it.

'This is it?' she probed when Joel came round to open the door for her.

Taking her arm, he steered her up the path and rang the doorbell. 'Relax, I'm not selling you off to white slavers.'

She shot him a scowl. 'Yes, but who lives here?'

'Are you always this impatient?' he countered, and they could hear halting footsteps approaching.

The door was opened by an elderly woman who had

once been beautiful and who, approaching eighty, was still striking. Her hair had once been the colour of autumn leaves, and was sadly faded, but there was sharpness in her green eyes.

'Good morning, Mrs Makepeace,' Joel greeted her warmly. 'I'm Joel Kendrick. We spoke on the telephone. Thank you for agreeing to see me today. I've brought someone with me who very much wants to meet you. This is Kathryn,' he said simply, stepping aside and urging Kathryn forward.

Still puzzled, but winging it, Kathryn smiled at the old woman, who gasped and raised a visibly trembling hand to her lips. 'How do you do? Your name is Makepeace? How strange, my mother's maiden name was Makepeace, too.'

The old lady scrabbled for a handkerchief and dabbed it at her eyes. Even so she smiled through tears that constantly welled up. 'Not so very strange, my dear. Your mother is my little girl. My little Lucy,' she revealed in a voice choked with emotion.

As Kathryn stood there, stunned, Joel carefully took the elderly woman by the arm and gently urged her back into the house. 'I think you'd feel better sitting down, Mrs Makepeace,' he decided, helping her into the compact sitting room. 'Close the door, would you, Kathryn?' he said over his shoulder, and, like an automaton, she did so, trailing along in his wake.

At the sitting-room door, she clutched onto the doorframe as she watched Joel lower the woman into a chair. It was incredible. This woman was her grandmother?

'You're really my grandmother?' Kathryn sought confirmation, her thoughts whirling madly.

Mrs Makepeace looked at her, her tears giving way to an expression of uncertainty. 'Yes, dear. I am.'

Kathryn shook her head helplessly. 'But how…? I don't understand!'

The other woman caught hold of Joel's hand as he straightened up. 'This young man came to find me,' she explained in a voice that still quavered with emotion.

Kathryn stared at Joel in amazement. 'You did?'

He placed a comforting hand on the older woman's shoulder as he responded. 'You said you wanted to meet her,' he said simply, as if that explained everything.

'I did. I do!' she exclaimed, knocked sideways by the knowledge that he would do this for her. Then she smiled encouragingly at the elderly woman as emotions rose to block her own throat. 'I've always wanted to meet you. Ever since I was a little girl.' Crossing the floor, she dropped to her knees before her grandmother and, this close, she could see the likeness to her own mother. She gently took hold of a hand riddled with arthritis. 'Forgive me for being surprised. I never expected this, but I really am most awfully pleased to meet you at last.'

Joel looked from one to the other, smiling faintly at the bright Titian locks of the one, and the faded remnants of the same colour of the other. 'I'll leave you two alone to get acquainted,' he said gently. 'If you need me, I'll be in the kitchen making tea,' he added, though neither was listening to him, and he went out unnoticed.

Alice Makepeace let out a shaky sigh. 'I can't quite believe this is happening myself. When your young man contacted me and explained who you were, and that you wanted to meet me—well, it was like a dream come true. I never thought it could happen. I thought you must all hate me.'

'Oh, no, not at all. Nobody hates you.' Kathryn refuted that quickly.

The older woman shook her head. 'That's not true. George hates me.' She referred to her ex-husband. 'And maybe Lucy does, too. I wouldn't blame her.'

Kathryn was compelled to honesty. 'Grandfather never forgave you, that's true. We don't get on, really. It's because I look a lot like you.'

Her grandmother nodded agreement. 'You do. Very much.'

'But Mother doesn't hate you,' Kathryn insisted. 'She's never had anything but sympathy for your situation. What hurts her is that she doesn't understand why you never kept in touch with her. What happened? Will you tell me?'

Alice looked beyond Kathryn, her thoughts lost in the past and far from pleasant. 'George happened. I never wanted to lose my daughter, but George's family had never approved of me. They helped him when he sued for custody, and when he won they helped him make it difficult for me to see Lucy. There were always excuses, reasons why a planned visit had to be postponed. In the end I realised they would never let me see her.'

Kathryn was appalled. 'Why didn't you take him to court? You had your rights!'

Alice sighed. 'Yes, I had my rights, but in those days it wasn't so easy. I had no family to help me, and no resources. In the end, so much time had passed I decided that Lucy was probably better off without me. Later, when my situation changed, there were so many times when I wanted to contact her. I wrote her letters I never posted. Found out where she lived and went to school. But I was a coward. I thought she must surely hate me for leaving her, so I did nothing. I let my daughter go without a fight, and I'll never forgive my-self for that.' Tears misted her eyes, and she looked away, pressing her hand to her lips.

Kathryn came to her feet quickly. Sinking onto the arm of the chair, she slipped her arm about the frail shoulders and hugged her. 'Please don't cry. You're not a coward. You'd just been hurt too much already. Mother knows that. She won't blame you, or hate you. Believe me. I know. She loves you. She always has.'

Alice Makepeace blinked up at her granddaughter hopefully. 'Do you really think so? I've missed her so much. If I could see her just once more, then all the pain would have been worth it. Do you think she would meet me, Kathryn?'

Kathryn smiled down into a face so much like her own. 'Of course she will. When I tell her that I've found you, she'll be on the telephone before you can blink.'

Her grandmother laughed, as Kathryn had wanted her to. 'How is she? Is she well? Is she happy?'

'Very well, very happy. You have four grandsons, too, you know.'

A light of interest entered those green eyes. 'Really? Tell me about them. Tell me about all of you,' she in-vited huskily, and with a laugh Kathryn drew up a chair and began to tell her all about the family she'd never known she had.

Almost an hour later Kathryn quietly entered the kitchen in search of the tea Joel had promised them. He was sitting at the small table reading a magazine he had found from somewhere. Her heart swelled with love for him for what he had done. Finding her grandmother for her. Crossing the room, she slipped her arms around his neck from behind and pressed a kiss to his cheek.

'Thank you,' she said huskily. 'You've made me very happy.'

Joel tossed the magazine onto the table and placed a hand over hers. 'That was my intention.'

'Well, it worked wonderfully,' she murmured with a decidedly watery smile. 'I don't know why you did it, but I'm glad you did.'

Joel eased her arms from over his head and drew her round onto his lap. 'I did it because I saw how important it was to you. It would make you happy, and making you happy suddenly seemed very important to me.'

Kathryn held her breath and searched his eyes. If she didn't know better, she could almost believe he loved her. It was the sort of thing a person would do for someone they loved.

She smiled bemusedly. 'I don't know how to thank you,' she confessed, and he quickly pressed a finger to her lips.

'Thanks aren't necessary. Seeing you happy is thanks enough. How is your grandmother?'

'She was very emotional, as you'd expect, but she handled it well. I think she could do with that tea now, and a rest to take it all in. It's a shock to the system to have your dreams come true like this.' She was still suffering aftershocks herself.

'It's all ready. We just have to boil the water again,' he responded, rising to his feet and settling her back on hers. 'Do you think she will be up to a trip to London today?' he asked as he switched on the kettle.

A light went on in Kathryn's mind and all became clear. 'She's the guest you're bringing to dinner?'

'It seemed the ideal solution, but if you think it would be too much…?'

Kathryn frowned uncertainly. 'I don't know. She's

not young any more. I'll ask her, but I have the feeling she would rather I paved the way first by telling my mother about her,' she ventured.

'You're probably right,' Joel conceded easily. The kettle boiled and he made the tea, carrying the tray through to the sitting room where Alice Makepeace sat with a bemused smile on her face.

As Kathryn had expected, when the suggestion was put to her that she come with them to meet her daughter she did not feel equal to the event. She needed time, and Kathryn understood that perfectly. She was still feeling the shock of surprise herself, and she was less than half this woman's age. Better to wait until her mother had been told, then the meeting could be planned, rather than thrust upon them.

They stayed with her grandmother for another couple of hours, listening to her reminisce. They weren't always comfortable memories, but they seemed to have a cathartic effect on the old lady. It was as if, by meeting Kathryn, a great weight had been lifted from her shoulders.

Eventually they had to leave, and Alice saw them to the door. There she caught Kathryn by the hand, and her eyes were twinkling. 'Your Joel must love you very much to have gone to so much trouble to find me for you,' she declared, winking at Joel, who grinned back.

'It's impossible not to love Kathryn,' he returned smoothly, and though she knew he was saying it solely for the old lady's benefit, colour dusted her cheeks.

'Now that we've found you, you must come to the wedding,' Kathryn invited, bending to kiss and hug the frail woman.

'I shall look forward to it,' Alice returned, smiling,

and it was with a full heart that Kathryn followed Joel
to the car and allowed him to help her inside.

She waved until the bungalow was out of sight, then
sat back with a sigh.

'Tired?' Joel asked, and she nodded.

'Emotionally more than physically. But I'm happy,
too.' She turned her head against the seat-back to look
at him. 'Thank you for lying,' she said softly, and he
cast her a questioning look. 'About loving me.'

Joel turned his gaze back to the road. 'Ah,' he said
shortly, and she smiled to herself.

'It was a kind thing to do, but then I've always
known you were kind. I guess it's one of the reasons
why I love you so much,' she went on with a soft laugh.

'Kathryn!' Joel exclaimed exasperatedly.

'I know, I know. You don't want to hear it. But
you're going to have to. What you did today only makes
me love you more.'

'That isn't what I meant,' he contested as they approached a crossroads. The traffic light was green as
they went through it.

Kathryn was just about to respond when out of the
corner of her eye she saw a car shooting the red lights
on her left. Alarm shot through her. 'Look out!' she
cried in terror, and then everything was a blur of light
and noise as the two cars collided. Her head hit something hard and everything went dark.

When Kathryn returned to the world again, her nose
told her where she was. That antiseptic smell could only
be a hospital. One look confirmed she *was* in a hospital
bed, but apart from having a raging thirst she seemed
fine, and all of her limbs moved when she tested them.
Her head ached when she attempted to raise it, and she

recalled hitting it just before blacking out. Memory of the accident returned, and with it an intense anxiety to know if Joel was all right.

This time she raised her head despite the queasiness the thumping brought with it. 'Joel?' she called out, just this side of panicking. The room was empty, though it was designed for four, and she had no sense of him. Oh, God! she thought wildly. He couldn't be dead! 'Joel!' she cried more sharply, scrabbling for the buzzer, needing to know.

'Kathryn?'

The sound of his voice calling her name brought her head round, and she felt such a wave of relief tears sprang to her eyes. The next second he came striding in from the corridor. He was minus his jacket, and there was blood on his shirt, the evidence of a cut on his cheek that was covered by a dressing.

Joel came directly to her, sitting on the edge of the bed and swooping her into his arms. They closed so tightly about her her breathing was restricted, but she didn't care. He was alive and well, and relieved tears trailed down her cheeks as she clung to him.

'I thought I'd lost you,' she declared brokenly.

Joel's hand cupped the back of her head, pressing her into his neck. 'When I saw you lying crumpled in the seat beside me, I thought I'd lost you, too,' he confessed thickly. 'I've never been so terrified in my whole life.'

Kathryn closed her eyes, sending up a silent prayer of thanks. 'What happened?' she asked 'I remember the car hitting us, then everything went black.' She felt him shudder.

'Fortunately for us the other car only winged us and spun us around. That's how you came to hit your head.

We were incredibly lucky that traffic was light. Had there been more... The other driver was well over the limit, apparently,' Joel explained, and she could hear his underlying anger.

Easing away, Kathryn checked out as much of him as she could with her eyes. 'You were hurt, too.' She pointed to his cheek.

'Just a scratch. It bled a lot, but it's not deep. You were the one we were worried about. You've been out for a while now, and they're going to keep you in overnight to check for concussion. I telephoned your parents and they insisted on coming up. Don't be surprised if your family arrive mob-handed,' he added dryly, and she chuckled—then wished she hadn't when her head thumped.

'They're very protective,' she reminded him unnecessarily.

'Well, they're going to have to learn to take a back seat. It's my job to protect you now,' he declared uncompromisingly. 'Not that I did too good a job today. When I saw that car heading right for you...'

'Hush!' Kathryn interrupted, pressing her hand over his lips. 'Don't think about it.'

Joel kissed her palm before reaching up and pulling it away. 'I have to. You see, it gave me the jolt I needed to be honest with myself at last. In that split second, when I thought I might lose you, the truth reared up and bit me. I suddenly knew I couldn't lose you. It was totally unacceptable.'

Kathryn's throat closed over at the blazing depth of feeling she could see in his eyes. It almost seemed as if he was saying... Her heart quailed at the thought. What if she was wrong? She wanted to believe her ears

and eyes weren't deceiving her, but dared not. To hope
and have that hope crushed would be too much on top
of everything else. She had to be certain before she
dared believe that a miracle was happening.

'Did you hit your head, too? You're not making
much sense, you know.' She tried to make light of it,
but her heart was racing fit to burst and her voice wob-
bled dangerously.

The tenderness in his touch as he reached out and ran
a finger gently along the fragile line of her jaw was
almost her undoing. 'I've been a fool. Worse, I've been
an arrogant fool. I thought I could command my heart
not to feel, but it knew better. Whilst my head was
telling me love doesn't exist, my heart was proving me
wrong.'

Kathryn's heart seemed to swell inside her as joy
burst its bounds. She wasn't mistaken. It was all right
to hope and believe. 'Joel—'

His hand cut her off. 'No, let me finish. I have to say
this and you deserve to hear it. When I was faced with
the possibility of a future without you in it, I finally
admitted to myself that I loved you. I've loved you for
a long time, it seems. In fact, I can't remember not
loving you. You walked into my life that day and
changed it for ever. My heart knew it, but my head
fought it. I'm sorry it's taken me so long to admit it.'

Though she felt like exploding with happiness, she
responded cautiously. 'Are you sure? Please be absolutely sure, because my happiness depends on it.'

Joel cupped his hands gently about her face. 'I'm a
man of my word and I won't renege. I told you once
to put me to the test, and I guess this is the moment of

truth. There is no doubt in my mind or my heart. I love you, Kathryn. I will always love you.'

Kathryn closed her eyes, drawing in a deep breath, a smile slowly spreading across her lips. When she looked at him again, her eyes blazed with love. 'I've longed to hear you say that, and thought I never would.'

'Do you trust me? Is my word enough?'

'Of course,' she sighed. 'I love you, and because I love you, I trust you.'

'In that case, there's one thing I have to ask you. Last time I did it, it was for all the wrong reasons. It was the easy option to ask you to marry me without admitting I loved you. Today I'm asking for no other reason than that I love you, and can't live without you. Will you marry me?' Joel asked in a voice made husky by emotion.

Her heart overflowed. 'Oh, yes,' she breathed happily.

'Thank God.' Joel's exclamation was heartfelt, and then he kissed her, carefully because of her head, but there was all the love in it that she could ever want.

'Did you really think I might say no this time?' Kathryn queried with a laugh.

Joel grimaced in self-mockery. 'Believe me, my hands were shaking almost as much as they were the evening I arrived to take you to dinner,' he confessed, and she looked at him in mild surprise.

'I didn't know that.'

His grin was shamefaced. 'I hid them in my pockets so you wouldn't see. I was so looking forward to seeing you again, I was very nearly a gibbering wreck. Something which had never happened to me since my very first date. That was the state you had me in.'

She would never have guessed. 'You hid it well.'

'So well that I hid the truth from myself.'

Kathryn rested her head on his shoulder, so completely happy it was almost like being slightly tipsy. 'Not any more, though.'

'No, not any more,' Joel agreed softly.

'When did you start to realise you loved me?' she wanted to know, and he laughed softly.

'You want your pound of flesh, don't you?' he drawled wryly. 'I guess it was when you described yourself as a faithful hound. Later I began to realise how jealous and possessive I felt about you. I wanted to see you happy, not hurt, and I was willing to take on your family to do it. The clincher was when you spoke of your successor waiting in the wings. I realised I didn't want anyone else. You were the only one for me.'

'So you asked me to marry you, and went off to find my grandmother for me. I'll have to start calling you my white knight.' Kathryn teased him with a full heart. She glanced up at him from the corner of her eye. 'Um—how long do you think we have before a nurse turns up to check on me?'

'Not too long, I should imagine,' he calculated wryly.

Her hand snaked up into his hair, tugging his head down. 'Then we'd better not waste any time. Kiss me again.'

'You know I could probably get thrown out of the hospital for this,' he warned, even as he complied.

'I'll risk it if you will,' she murmured seductively, and he gave that chuckle which melted her bones.

'Are you flirting with me, sweetheart?'

'If you can't tell, I'm not doing it right,' she breathed

against his lips. 'Come on, Big Bad Wolf, do your worst.'

Smiling male lips brushed hers. 'Wolves mate for life, you know.'

Kathryn nipped at his bottom lip with her small white teeth. 'Hmm, I like the sound of that.'

'Somehow I thought you might,' Joel growled, and finally, most satisfyingly, kissed her.

MILLS & BOON®

Makes any time special™

Mills & Boon publish 29 new titles every month. Select from...

Modern Romance™   Tender Romance™

Sensual Romance™

Medical Romance™ Historical Romance™

MAT2

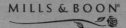

MILLS & BOON®

Modern Romance™

DUARTE'S CHILD by Lynne Graham

Only days before she gave birth, Emily left her husband, Duarte de Monteiro. Now Duarte has traced her and his baby son, and brought them back to Portugal. But has he done so because he loves her, or just because he wants his son?

THE UNFORGETTABLE HUSBAND by Michelle Reid

For a year Samantha had been existing with amnesia, but when a dark, imposing man walked into her life, she knew her past was about to be revealed. Andre Visconte insisted he was her husband. But why hadn't he found her until now?

THE HOT-BLOODED GROOM by Emma Darcy

When Bryce Templar met Sunny at a conference the attraction between them was like a bolt of electricity. He wanted Sunny, and needed an heir—but would there be more to their marriage than a baby bargain?

THE PROSPECTIVE WIFE by Kim Lawrence

Matt Devlin is the ultimate millionaire playboy. His family are constantly trying to find him a wife, so he is instantly suspicious when blonde, beautiful Kat turns up as his physiotherapist! The attraction is instantaneous…

On sale 3rd August 2001

Available at most branches of WH Smith, Tesco, Martins, Borders, Easons, Sainsbury, Woolworth and most good paperback bookshops 0701/01a

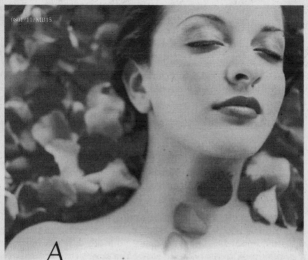

A
Perfect Family

An enthralling family saga by bestselling author

PENNY
JORDAN

Published 20th July

4 FREE

books and a surprise gift!

We would like to take this opportunity to thank you for reading this Mills & Boon® book by offering you the chance to take FOUR more specially selected titles from the Modern Romance™ series absolutely FREE! We're also making this offer to introduce you to the benefits of the Reader Service™—

* ★ FREE home delivery
* ★ FREE gifts and competitions
* ★ FREE monthly Newsletter
* ★ Exclusive Reader Service discounts
* ★ Books available before they're in the shops

Accepting these FREE books and gift places you under no obligation to buy, you may cancel at any time, even after receiving your free shipment. Simply complete your details below and return the entire page to the address below. *You don't even need a stamp!*

YES! Please send me 4 free Modern Romance books and a surprise gift. I understand that unless you hear from me, I will receive 6 superb new titles every month for just £2.49 each, postage and packing free. I am under no obligation to purchase any books and may cancel my subscription at any time. The free books and gift will be mine to keep in any case.

P1ZEA

Ms/Mrs/Miss/Mr ....Initials......................................

BLOCK CAPITALS PLEASE

Surname ....

Address ....

....

....Postcode................................

Send this whole page to:
UK: FREEPOST CN81, Croydon, CR9 3WZ
EIRE: PO Box 4546, Kilcock, County Kildare (stamp required)